"Good night,

He stopped and turned around to face h...n. Good night." Slowly, one hand rose. Almost hesitantly he brushed her cheek with his thumb.

Natasha felt her eyes go wide. If this had been a movie, it would have been the perfect time for the tall, dark, handsome hero to kiss the damsel in distress. Not that she was in distress. He'd fed her and she felt fine now, except for being so tired she could hardly stand.

He looked down at her mouth as though he was thinking about kissing her.

For the past year, this was the moment she'd dreamed about—fantasized about—because she knew it would never happen.

Books by Gail Sattler

Love Inspired Heartsong Presents

The Best Man's Secret
The Best Man's Holiday Romance

GAIL SATTLER,

an award-winning author of more than forty books, lives in Vancouver, BC (where you don't have to shovel rain), with her husband, three sons, two dogs and a lizard who is quite cuddly for a reptile. Gail enjoys making music with a local jazz band and a community orchestra. When she's not writing or making music, Gail likes to sit back with a hot coffee and a good book.

GAIL SATTLER

The Best Man's Holiday Romance

HEARTSONG
PRESENTS

Recycling programs
for this product may
not exist in your area.

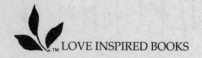 LOVE INSPIRED BOOKS

ISBN-13: 978-0-373-48738-7

The Best Man's Holiday Romance

Copyright © 2014 by Gail Sattler

www.Harlequin.com

Printed in U.S.A.

Love is patient, love is kind. It does not envy, it does not boast, it is not proud. It does not dishonor others, it is not self-seeking, it is not easily angered, it keeps no record of wrongs. Love does not delight in evil but rejoices with the truth.

—*1 Corinthians* 13:4–6

To my husband, Tim, who is always my biggest muse.

Chapter 1

As the bride worked to pull the keeper section out of the bouquet, Natasha Brickson scanned the crowd of ladies.

She'd heard that five hundred people had been invited, so that meant probably half of the two hundred and fifty ladies present were gathering to catch the bouquet.

The bride and groom had four attendants each. The wedding had been organized by a professional planner, and the hall, booked a year in advance, had been professionally decorated.

She would never have a wedding like this.

Since she didn't feel the same excitement as the rest of the crowd, Natasha stepped back from the festivities to find herself beside the wedding cake. The five-layer cake was topped by dolls that looked exactly like the bride and groom, including a miniature replica of Crystal's dress.

She would never have a dress like Crystal's, either.

That was because she would never have a wedding. Ever.

As she turned away from the cake, she found herself looking right at the reason, standing against the wall, away from the crowd.

Jeff Shaw, the best man.

She'd loved him for the past year, but any relationship with him was not to be.

Jeff was in love with her sister, Heather, and four weeks from today, Jeff and Heather would be married.

Looking beyond the mob of anxious single ladies, Natasha glanced around. She still didn't see her sister. In fact, she hadn't seen Heather all day.

The activity of the moment was the bride getting ready to throw her bouquet, so all attention was focused on Crystal and her bridesmaids.

Natasha, however, watched Jeff, standing alone, away from everyone, looking forlorn instead of happy as he should have been. She'd have thought he'd be watching along with Heather and making last-minute plans for their wedding, which would be very similar, except with about half the number of guests.

Last weekend had been Natasha's best friend, Ashley's, wedding. In comparison to the head count here, which rivaled the population of a small town, only nine people had attended Ashley and Dave's wedding, and that included the bride and groom.

Instead of a gown that cost over a month's salary—before deductions—Ashley had used her mother's vintage dress, which only needed to be hemmed. With no time to order a fancy wedding cake, they'd got one from Costco, and the small reception had been at the home of Dave's best friend.

Her friend's wedding was the most romantic thing she'd ever seen. Even the groom cried.

Out of the three women present Natasha had been the only one not married, so Ashley had simply handed her the bouquet.

"Is everyone ready?" Crystal called out as she turned around, waving the gorgeous bouquet over her head, enticing the ladies who rivaled a mob waiting for the doors at the mall to open on Black Friday.

Natasha stepped farther back. She didn't need a second bouquet to rub it in her face that she was never going to get married.

Crystal tossed the bouquet over her head.

When the bouquet flew way up in the air, everyone gasped as it barely missed the chandelier, arced over the throng of eager single women and hit one of the ceiling fans. Thrown off its trajectory, it flew straight toward Natasha.

She had to catch it or it would land on the floor.

A few women cast her dirty looks, but most of them congratulated her, even though acquiring it hadn't been a challenge.

Natasha forced herself to smile while she again looked around the room for her sister.

Instead, her eyes caught Jeff. As the men gathered

to catch the garter, Jeff backed up until he was leaning against the wall.

All his best-man duties had come to an end and he should have been joining in the fun. Instead, he continued to stand back, which wasn't like him. Come to think of it, he hadn't been his usual self all day.

Bouquet in hand, she approached him.

"Hi, Jeff. You look quite dashing. But I suppose you've heard that a lot today."

One hand rose to the bow tie. "Not really."

She waited for him to say how much he hated wearing a tuxedo, but he didn't. He didn't even complain about the bow tie.

Her heart clenched with the visual. Soon he'd be wearing another tuxedo, when he said "I do" to her sister. Natasha didn't know how she was going to survive being the maid of honor, but she had to go through the motions.

"The wedding went really smooth, don't you think?" she asked, rather than let the silence hang.

Jeff looked away, not to the gathering of men, but to the door. "Yeah."

Natasha's attention was naturally drawn to the bride and groom, where Luis was pulling the garter off Crystal's leg in slow motion, looking as though he was quite enjoying the process. Most of the men surrounding them hooted, and a few whistled.

"I guess there's not much point to you joining all the men, is there? Pretty soon you'll be doing the same thing."

He stiffened and spoke without looking at her. "No. I won't."

She smiled. "Of course you will. Heather even showed me the garter she's going to wear. Where is Heather, anyway?"

"She's not here."

"Why not? Is she sick?" Last night Heather had seemed a little distracted, but otherwise fine.

"No. She's not sick."

Natasha laid the bouquet on the table beside her, and rested her hand on Jeff's arm. "I don't understand."

"I told her not to come. She's been cheating on me."

Natasha's heart froze at the pain in his voice. "That can't be true. She's been making me dizzy with wedding preparations."

The muscles in his arm tensed. "When I got to the apartment to pick her up, as I stepped out of the elevator I caught her in the hallway kissing your married neighbor. The wedding's off. Now, if you'll excuse me."

Before she could think of something to say, Jeff pulled his arm away and strode off.

"No! Jeff!" Abandoning the bouquet on the table, she ran after him. "Wait!"

He spun around to face her. "What?" he spat out.

"Are you sure?" The second the words left her lips she realized what a stupid question she'd asked. She pressed her fingers to her temples. "I'm sorry. Of course you're sure. What happened?"

He let out a defeated sigh. "I caught them together just outside the door, wrapped in each other's arms with their tongues down each other's throats. It was obviously not a one-time indiscretion."

Natasha's stomach clenched into a painful knot. "What did she say?"

Jeff shrugged his shoulders. "There was nothing she could say. I demanded my ring back, and left." He ran one hand over his breast pocket, then rammed it in his pants pocket. "Now that I think about it, a lot of loose ends are coming together. This has been going on for months, and everything went right over my head."

Comments Heather had made about their neighbors clicked into place. Especially about knowing when Melissa, Zac's wife, wasn't going to be home.

It was true. And she hadn't seen it. "I don't know what to say."

Jeff dragged his free hand over his face. "Yeah, well, life goes on. Excuse me. I need some fresh air."

Before she could say anything more, he turned and strode outside.

All she could do was stare at the closed door. Her heart broke for him. She couldn't imagine what he'd been going through for the past few hours. Until now, he'd held himself together so well no one would know anything was wrong.

She wanted to think that Heather wouldn't do such a thing, but that wouldn't have been honest. Typically self-centered, her sister often put her wants over the needs and feelings of others. Heather always knew how to get everything she wanted, and the cost was never an issue.

They'd met Jeff on the same day, and both of them

developed an instant crush on him. Knowing Natasha
was interested upped Heather's pursuit. Heather was
naturally charming and knew how to attract men easily, while Natasha had always been shy—at least, she
had been back then.

Rather than fight with her sister over a man, Natasha had stepped back, waiting for the day Heather and
Jeff broke up. Often Heather hadn't been ready when
Jeff arrived to take her out, obligating Natasha to keep
him company until Heather appeared. It hadn't taken
long for Natasha to fall in love with him. She'd told
herself that her love for him was strong enough to wait
for when he was free of a relationship—especially a
relationship with her sister. But that never happened.
In record time, Heather and Jeff had become engaged.

Even though he was still in love with her sister, it
broke her heart to see him like this.

She didn't know what she was going to do to help
him, but she was going to do something.

Still in his pajamas, Jeff stood staring into his closet.
He couldn't believe it. He was going to church alone.

If Heather was there, he didn't know how he would
face her.

Instead of picking a shirt, Jeff squeezed his eyes
shut and stood still.

Most Sunday mornings when he arrived to pick
Heather up, Tasha was just leaving and Heather was
nowhere near ready. Often by the time she was ready,
she'd felt it too disruptive to walk into the church sanc-

tuary after the service started, so they just went out for an early lunch instead.

Many times he had the feeling she really didn't want to go, but only went to church because he did. He doubted Heather would go to church alone today, so he probably wouldn't see her.

Except walking in alone, people were bound to notice that she was missing and ask where she was. He wasn't ready to talk about it—not while the hurt was so fresh. More than just fresh, the wound was still bleeding.

He just didn't understand.

He'd been a good and attentive partner. Whenever Heather had done something he didn't like, instead of complaining he bit his tongue and let it ride unless it was something really important. Every once in a while he bought her little gifts just to show her she was special, and he remembered her birthday without needing to be reminded.

This wasn't the first time the same thing had happened to him. Even though he hadn't been on the verge of walking down the aisle with Kate, their relationship was supposed to be exclusive. A mutual friend told him that Kate had been seeing someone else at the same time. Aware that he knew, Kate had sent him a Dear John text, taken him off her friends list, and that was the end of that. It had hurt, but not as bad as this.

He'd had plans to marry Heather—to devote himself to being her partner for life.

Without picking a shirt, Jeff turned and crossed the

room, parted the blinds and stared out the window at the trees just starting to turn to their autumn colors.

What was the matter with him? He thought he was a decent guy. He wasn't a hotshot millionaire executive, but he had a good reputation for his skills as a journeyman plumber. He liked his job and made good money without endless hours of overtime. Most people liked him. He went to church almost every Sunday. He was nice to children, and he didn't kick puppies.

As he stared outside, a familiar car slowed in front of his house, pulled to the side and stopped.

Tasha's car. Heather's sister.

She didn't get out, though.

His phone rang. He knew who it would be, but answered, anyway.

"Hey there," Tasha's voice rang out much too cheerfully. "I was wondering if you were going to church this morning, and if you needed a ride."

"Why would I need a ride? There's nothing wrong with my car."

"I just happened to be passing by and thought I'd save you the gas."

Since he knew exactly where she lived he also knew his house wasn't between Tasha and Heather's apartment and the church. And she knew that as a journeyman plumber, he made good money, so he didn't have to worry about two dollars' worth of gas.

He looked down at his pajama-clad legs and wiggled his bare toes. "I'm not ready."

A pause hung on the line for a few seconds. "I've got an idea. I want to go to my friend Ashley's church, but I don't want to go alone. It's close to your place, so there's still lots of time. Will you come with me?"

"Why don't you sit with your friend?"

"She's not going to be there today. She's gone on…" Tasha's voice hung for a few seconds. "She's out of town today. But I want to check it out. It's really small and I thought it would be a nice change." She paused again. "Neither of us will know anyone."

Going someplace where no one knew him did have somewhat of an appeal. He dragged one hand down the front of his pajamas. "That might be a good idea, but I'm not dressed yet."

"We've got lots of time. I'm going down the street to get us some coffee and a couple of muffins. I can't talk on the phone while I'm driving. I'll be back in about ten minutes. Bye."

The phone was dead and her car was moving before he could take a breath to tell her he would probably need a little more time. He hit the button to call back and got a recording that she was unavailable as her taillights disappeared around the corner.

Jeff sighed and put the phone down. In all the time he'd spent with Tasha when he was waiting for Heather to get ready, he'd come to know her fairly well, so this didn't surprise him. She planned everything to the minutest detail, and always followed her plans. He didn't know how she knew he wouldn't be ready, but she had a plan B, or maybe it was even plan A.

Unless he got dressed quickly, both of them were going to be pretty embarrassed when she returned.

He went back to the closet to grab a clean shirt

and a pair of jeans without a hole and had the fastest shower on record. He'd just finished brushing his teeth when the doorbell rang.

When he opened the door to let her in, he froze, unable to release the doorknob.

It was almost like letting Heather in; they looked so alike. Of course since they were sisters it was natural. He hadn't thought about it before, but suddenly it felt…unsettling.

Still unable to move, he told himself not to think of ways they were similar, but to think about the ways they were different.

Tasha wore her hair in a ponytail so no hair blocked her face. Also, her hair was longer, had a slight wave, and even though it was the same light brown, Tasha's didn't have as many different colors in it. The lighter parts were natural, from the sun, not like Heather's, since she spent a lot of time and money at the salon. He actually liked the natural look better, but he couldn't have told Heather that.

Both sisters had the same dark brown eyes, except that Tasha didn't wear as much makeup, so they seemed more…normal. While she wasn't gorgeous like some of the actresses on television, she was pretty in a nice, wholesome way. Nothing particularly striking, but well-balanced.

Most of all, she had a really nice smile, and it always felt sincere. When she smiled her whole face lit up and her eyes almost sparkled.

Except this morning Tasha's smile seemed uncharacteristically cheery, which meant he probably looked uncharacteristically crabby.

"Come on in, Tasha," he muttered, trying to sound gracious as he released the doorknob and stepped back.

Her smiled wavered for a second, then returned.

Tasha handed him a hot cup. "Double double. I remember how you take it. I hope you like blueberry muffins. That's what I got for you."

"That's perfect. Thanks," he said as she walked past him.

"I've never been to your place before. Where's the kitchen?"

He felt himself blush. He'd never been rude; his mother had raised him better than that. Yet today, his usual good manners had left him.

Jeff pointed down the hall as he closed the door behind her. "That way. Sorry."

Once in the kitchen he pulled out a chair for her, then seated himself. After inhaling the aroma of the fresh muffins, Jeff's stomach made an embarrassing gurgle. He looked down as he reached into the bag, then began to peel the paper off one of the muffins. "Sorry. I didn't realize I was so hungry."

"No worries. I figure we have about twenty minutes before we need to go. Lots of time. Enjoy."

No awkward silence hung between them as they ate their impromptu breakfast because there was no silence. Tasha talked nonstop—something he'd never experienced with her before. Not that he had anything worthwhile to contribute. In a way, the distraction was good, because in order to pay attention he couldn't wallow in his own misery.

As soon as Tasha finished her last bite she checked her watch, pushed her chair out and stood. "Let's go." Without allowing him a chance to respond she turned and started toward the door, giving him no choice but to follow.

She waited for him to lock the door, then headed for her car parked on the street, versus his car in the carport.

It would be rude if he suggested they take his car after she'd made a point about saving him gas money, so he said nothing. After the service he would take her out for lunch, and he'd pick up the bill.

Chapter 2

As they headed for the church, Jeff turned to Tasha. "Now that we're on the way, I'm thinking that neither of us is going to know anyone there. You said this place is going to be really small. How small?"

"I'm not sure. The building isn't large—it could probably seat about two hundred—but I've never been there for a service. From what Ashley said, I think there will be about a hundred people there this morning."

At his church, around seven hundred people attended the early and late services. In a group as small as this, it wouldn't be possible to simply get lost in the crowd, because there would be no crowd. However, no one would ask about his upcoming ex-wedding.

Monday he'd go back to work, where the first

thing he'd do was cancel his vacation. Opening up that prime slot for someone else would raise questions about why he didn't need it anymore, but staying home would remind him every day that he hadn't flown off to the Bahamas in marital bliss. He didn't want to wallow, so he was best off where he could be busy, and that was at work. He didn't know what Heather wanted to do with the honeymoon package she'd booked and paid for, but told himself he didn't care.

Visions of the woman who would have been his wife and her married boyfriend danced through his mind. He didn't know if that made him more angry or depressed, and it was an odd feeling.

"Jeff? Are you okay?"

Realizing he'd been staring at Tasha without really seeing her, he turned to look out the car window. "Sorry. I was just thinking about stuff I've got to cancel and see if I can get the deposits back. Heather booked the honeymoon, but everything else is on my credit card so it's up to me to cancel it."

He wasn't looking at Tasha, but he heard her sharp intake of breath. He looked left to right at the traffic, but didn't see anything coming toward them out of control.

He turned toward her. "What's wrong?"

"Heather will probably ask me to cancel all the honeymoon stuff. I'll refuse, and then she'll probably get all dramatic, hoping I cave."

That wouldn't surprise him. "I know she got some pricey packages. I don't know if she bought cancellation insurance." He couldn't remember what he'd paid cancellation fees for, but he supposed he'd find out the hard way. "We booked most of the wedding with my credit card, including the flowers." He lowered his head and covered his face with his hands. "One at a time it didn't seem like so much, but now that I think of it, there's a lot of stuff that I'm going to be responsible to cancel. Everything except for the flights and hotel package and her dress. I should probably take tomorrow off, just to make all the phone calls."

"Most of the vendors will have voice mail. Start calling today and leave your email for them to contact you back."

"That's probably a good idea." He didn't want to stay home tomorrow and stare at his walls. That would drive him crazy.

Tasha flicked on the turn signal, and the car slowed. "Here we are."

As she turned into the lot Jeff mentally did a rough count on the number of cars, which indicated that there would probably be about a hundred people there, not including children.

He checked the time. It was five minutes to the hour, so most people should be going in to secure a good seat. However, with a small number of people, there were bound to be a lot of empty seats, so no one would need to hurry.

Once in the parking spot, Tasha turned off the car and grabbed her purse. Jeff sat back in the seat to wait, figuring she'd check her makeup in the rear-view mirror and reapply her lipstick the way her sister always did.

"What are you doing?" Tasha dropped her keys into her purse and pushed her door open. "We have to go. I hate walking in late."

Jeff opened his door at the same time as Tasha's door closed behind her. She hadn't even glanced in the mirror.

He had to rush to catch up to her. She walked at a quick pace to the door, then slowed as they stepped inside.

"This is…cozy…" he muttered as he looked around. The building was old and small and showed the wear of the combination of time and maintenance. Despite the time, people stood in small circles chatting and drinking coffee.

A really tall young man broke away from the group nearest to the door and approached them, extending one hand with a church bulletin. "Welcome to Saint Nick's. I've never seen you here before. I'm glad you could come." He glanced around at everyone else standing around, and when no one moved, he looked back toward them. "Do you see anyone you know?"

Tasha shook her head. "No, but we do know Dave and Ashley."

The man's eyes widened "You know Dave?"

Tasha smiled and nodded. "I'm good friends with Ashley, so naturally I know Dave, but I know Ashley better."

"Dave's a great guy." The man turned and looked at Jeff, as if waiting for him to say something great about Dave. Jeff had never met Dave, but he didn't want to get into a discussion or make excuses. He just wanted to go into the sanctuary and sit down. Alone. Jeff nodded, pretty sure Dave had to be a great guy if he married Tasha's best friend.

"My name's Cory. Let me show you in."

Jeff and Tasha followed Cory into the sanctuary and slid into a pew near the back. At one minute to the hour, everyone who had been standing in the foyer yakking flooded in and found seats. The last person sat just as the worship leader and the band walked in.

Jeff knew most of the songs, so he felt pretty comfortable with the worship. The only awkward thing was that instead of Heather, Tasha was beside him. Unlike Heather, Tasha belted out all the songs at a good volume, not caring that she missed a few notes. During one of the songs he thought he saw tears in her eyes, but the worship leader asked everyone to bow their heads in prayer before he could be sure. Instead of paying attention to Tasha, he listened to the worship leader's prayer, and joined the congregation in a heartfelt "Amen" at the end.

He settled in to listen to the pastor's sermon, noting when the pastor asked the congregation to follow along as he read a Bible verse, about half of the people pulled out electronic devices, and half used an actual book.

Tasha pulled a tablet out of her purse to follow along, while he had his Bible on his cell phone. Overall, the pastor was a good speaker and covered his subject matter well. Jeff was almost sorry when it was over, and wondered if maybe he'd come back.

After the service was finished they made their way into the foyer. At the back a large coffee urn sat at the edge of a table, along with cups, condiments and a few boxes of doughnuts.

He'd heard of such things at small churches, but never experienced it.

Beside him, Tasha slowed her step. "Do you want to stay and visit with these people, or do you want to leave?"

He hadn't intended to do any more than listen to the sermon, but before he could open his mouth, Cory and a few more men approached them. "I hear you know Dave," one of them said. "I heard Dave and Ashley got married last weekend."

Tasha nodded. "It was kind of fast, but they didn't want to wait."

"I guess they're on their honeymoon, because they're not here."

Tasha smiled. "Ashley said they wanted to stay away from crowds, so they went camping in the mountains."

A slideshow of the pictures of the resort in the Bahamas he'd looked at with Heather flashed through his mind. Sandy beaches, young couples in bathing suits relaxing in the sunshine. Candlelight meals and drinks with pretty paper umbrellas on beachside patio tables. At night, lounging in the luxurious hotel pool, with fluffy plush towels and wraps neatly folded on lounge chairs for when they were done. That was a honeymoon. Not huddling around a fire in the middle of nowhere, fighting swarms of bugs until bedtime and then worrying if a raccoon was going to steal all the food in the middle of the night.

Suddenly Jeff wanted to be away from this discussion of honeymoons and happily-ever-afters. While he was glad Tasha's friend was having a good time, he didn't want to be reminded of what had been stripped away from him.

One of the men shrugged his shoulders. "I've never heard of anyone going camping for their honeymoon before. Especially since Ashley is freshly out of a cast."

Jeff doubted they planned to do much hiking on their honeymoon, but discretion made him hold his tongue.

Tasha grinned. "Ashley and Dave like to take pictures of nature, so that's what they're doing."

"That sounds like a strange honeymoon," another man said, "but if that's what they want, good for them."

Jeff's gut clenched. At least they were having a honeymoon. The cool weather would keep them close together, and maybe that was their plan all along.

"They should be back tonight. I know she has to go to work tomorrow. She could only get a week off."

Jeff had booked three weeks off. Two for the honeymoon, and one week to get settled together.

So much for that.

Tasha looked at him, then back to Cory. "I'm really sorry, but we need to leave now. Maybe we'll see you again next week."

He shook Cory's hand. "Nice meeting you."

The second they were inside Tasha's car, she said, "I'm so sorry. I didn't know anyone was going to corner me and ask about Ashley and Dave on their honeymoon."

"It's okay. Let's go…" He almost said *home*, but then remembered the mental promise he'd made—that he was going to take Tasha out for lunch in exchange for using her gas. She'd meant well trying to distract him from his troubles, so he couldn't hold the conversation topic with strangers against her. Besides, he really didn't want to go home to stare at the walls and think of what happened. The vision of Heather locked in the arms of another man was too close to recent memory. He would rather keep busy. Tomorrow, he would start to deal with it. "Let's go out for lunch. My treat."

"Really? You don't have to pay for me."

He'd always paid for Heather, but he wasn't going to tell Tasha that. "I know I don't have to. I'm going to because I want to. Pick your favorite place, and let's go."

"I can't argue with that. You're on."

Natasha drove out of the church parking lot, but she didn't know where to go. When she'd arrived at Jeff's door she could tell he was still shell-shocked. Taking him to the strange environment of a different church had helped pull him away from himself, at least for a little while. When people he didn't know started talking about Ashley and Dave's wedding, she realized she'd made a mistake, and made their escape as soon as she could.

Being where something else could distract him was what he needed. Just the two of them in a private setting of a restaurant might make it too easy to talk about Heather, and she didn't think he was ready for that quite yet.

The next choice would be her apartment, because she knew she had enough food in the fridge to make a nice lunch. However, with that option came the chance that Heather would come home from wherever it was she'd gone, and that couldn't happen. The next time she saw her sister, with or without Jeff, Natasha feared she might be tempted to scratch her sister's eyes out, and that wasn't a very Christian thing to do. Especially on a Sunday when she'd just been to church. Fortunately, the pastor's theme hadn't been forgiveness, but it was still something she needed to work on.

They definitely couldn't go to Jeff's house, where reminders of his canceled wedding were strewn about. They needed to go to a place he'd never been, to make a complete break from his usual life. Tomorrow everything would hit him between the eyes, and there was nothing she could do about that. Right now, she wanted to take him away from his troubles.

For today, she just wanted to be his friend because he needed one—his best friend, Luis, was away on his own honeymoon, and the rest of his friends were probably having a postparty meltdown.

Actually, she didn't want to be merely Jeff's friend. Not long ago she'd wanted to be where Heather had been—at his side as his soul mate, and maybe one day his wife.

Stopped at a red light and waiting for the turning arrow, she studied Jeff as discreetly as she could.

She'd known him for a couple of years, and she'd probably loved him for half of that time.

While he probably wasn't the most handsome man in the universe, he was close—at least in her eyes. His strong chin matched his nose, which maybe was a little big, but it just made him that much more masculine. His dark brown hair was highlighted with a bit of copper from the summer sun, beginning to fade, but still striking, especially in combination with his dusty-blue eyes. When he smiled, the start of crow's-feet appeared at the corners of his eyes, indicating that he smiled a lot. As a plumber he used a lot of heavy tools, so he was muscular, and even better, his muscles were natural from real work, not merely firm from working in the gym once a week. Slightly taller than average, he had big feet, which she often teased him about. He always laughed at her comments, showing those delightful little crow's-feet, which made her fall in love with him a bit more every time.

But of course he wasn't laughing now.

"I have an idea," she said as she made the left turn. "Instead of going to a restaurant, how would you like to get a couple of hot dogs and take a walk in the park? We can stop at 7-Eleven and buy a loaf of bread and feed the ducks that haven't flown south."

He turned toward her and smiled—it was a smile, but a sad smile. It almost made her cry.

"Most of our ducks have flown to California. What we'll see is the nonmigratory species, and the ones that have flown south from Alaska. To them, Washington State is south. We'll most likely see goldeneyes and mallards and wigeons, but if we're lucky, maybe we'll see some mergansers."

She smiled back. She had no idea he was a duck aficionado. "I think that's a yes?"

He shrugged his shoulders. "Sure. Are you dressed for a walk?"

"Of course I am, or I wouldn't have suggested it." The second the words came out of her mouth, she realized why he'd asked. Even when wearing jeans, Heather always wore four-inch heels. If Natasha had been wearing such things to church, they would have needed to go home to change. Although, really, she didn't own anything like that. She did a lot of standing and walking at work, and she refused to wear ridiculous heels.

As well, because she'd planned to spend the day with Jeff she'd dressed comfortably, and that included her usual sensible footwear.

She pulled into the nearest gas station with a convenience store, and Jeff ran in to get a loaf of bread. Except he came out with two iced drinks and a bag, which he held open for her to view the contents.

"You've got not just the bread, but also two bags of chips, two sandwiches and two chocolate bars."

He nodded. "Now we can go straight to the park. I don't have my camera—do you have yours?"

"You know I do." She always kept her small point-and-shoot and an extra battery in her purse so she could take hundreds of photos on a moment's notice. Many people teased her about it, but she was the one everyone came to when they wanted a photo. "You can take pictures with your cell phone if you want."

"I guess," he said as he took a long slurp from his straw, then slipped the drink into the holder. "But a real camera is easier to download. And you have a real camera."

"If you can call a digital real. One day I want to get a real film camera."

"And a shop to develop the film, too, I assume? Where does a person go to even buy real film anymore, or get it developed?"

She shrugged her shoulders. "I have no idea. Bad idea. Let's go."

Jeff didn't say much as they continued on to the park, but at least he now was adding something to the conversation, and she considered that a good sign. Before they went to church she'd barely got a word out of him. Not that he would get over the breakup of his relationship with Heather in such a short time, but it gave her hope. If she had to stereotype Jeff, she would call him the strong and silent type of guy. He usually wasn't a talker, but when he was upset, he went silent to the extreme. She'd taken enough management courses to know that it was better to keep the conversation going, even if he didn't talk about what was bothering him. Which meant she had to steer him to topics that interested him.

She had a feeling that once they arrived at their destination, she was going to learn a lot about ducks.

Chapter 3

Jeff tossed his hard hat into his locker, and unfastened his tool belt.

His first day back on the job as a newly single man had been an eye-opener. Not only had he learned a little about some of his coworkers, he also learned a lot about human nature.

When everyone heard that the wedding was off, after the expected manly condolences, comments were made not only about Jeff being single, but also that Heather was now single. A number of the guys had asked for her phone number and if he minded them going out with his ex. He'd cringed at the concept. Despite the reason for the breakup, having someone he knew go out with her just felt too invasive. After he told them the reason he'd split up with Heather, all of the guys changed their minds except one. Frank claimed that as long as he knew they wouldn't be exclusive, he didn't care; he only wanted a good time, not a commitment with a ball and chain.

At that comment, most of them laughed, but still, no one else asked for her number.

One of them had wanted Heather's sister's number, which had made him strangely angry.

He didn't give anyone any numbers.

Now that the guys were all on their way to wherever they went on a Monday night, he was alone. Since he had nowhere to go and no one to see, Jeff didn't mind being the last one out or to lock everything up and secure the compound.

After he'd checked everything was put away for the night, he pulled his cell out of his pocket to order a pizza to pick up on the way home, and noticed a new text message.

It was Tasha saying she was picking up a pizza and would meet him back at his place in half an hour to help him cancel wedding arrangements.

He poked through his phone, trying to find Tasha's phone number in his call log so he could call her and tell her not to come. Yesterday he hadn't been good company, and he wasn't going to be any better today. He'd been sullen during the church service, and then once they got to the park he couldn't stop talking about duck habitats and migrations. They'd picked up Chinese takeout for supper, then gone back to his place, where instead of going through what needed to be canceled, he'd remained in duck mode.

When he was in his teens he'd come across a cat that had captured and nearly killed a baby duck. He'd saved the duck, nursed her back to health and then kept her as a pet since she couldn't be released into the wild because she couldn't fly and she had a permanent limp—which for a duck was pretty sad. It didn't matter that she couldn't walk right, but she couldn't swim in a straight line, either.

Jeff bowed his head and pinched the bridge of his nose. He hadn't told any of his adult friends about Daffodil. Heather didn't even know. When he'd introduced Heather to his parents they'd met at his house, not at his parents' place, where Daffodil still lived. Since they'd been just recently engaged the topic of his pet duck hadn't come up. But not only had he told Tasha, he'd shown her pictures.

Then he'd explained that because Daffodil couldn't fly, he'd needed to take her into the house in the winter. But since ducks couldn't be house-trained like cats or dogs, his mother had started sewing duck diapers after being inspired by pictures she'd found on the internet. The diapers had worked so well that even though they looked ridiculous, his mother fancied them up, then started a home-based business selling fancy duck diapers on eBay, and that had later financed a large part of his college tuition.

While his mother had been sewing duck diapers, he'd designed and constructed a number of waterways for Daffodil. He'd also designed some for the wildlife center, where he'd had a part-time job when he got older. His friends had teased him that since he'd had such fun with pipes and fittings he should be a plumber when he grew up, and that had indeed been his career choice.

His life was what it was because of a dipsy duck that wore designer diapers.

It even sounded stupid.

It was no wonder he couldn't hold down a decent relationship.

He stared at the phone in his hand. There was no point in phoning to tell Tasha to not come. He had a feeling she would have her phone already turned off. He'd learned that from experience already.

He texted a quick Thx, just in case she actually looked, slipped the phone into his pocket and made his way to his car. When he was a block from home, as he made the last turn he found himself driving behind Tasha.

Another day, he would have smiled at his good timing. For tonight, nothing was good. Tonight the plans for his life were going to swirl into a deep pit, along with a fair amount of his savings from nonrefundable deposits.

She pulled over in front of his house, allowing him to go ahead of her to park his car in the carport, then she pulled in behind him.

Pizza in hand, Tasha met him at the door. "What great timing."

"I guess," he said, feeling as if he should say something, but he didn't know what.

He led her into the kitchen, which fortunately he'd cleaned since yesterday's meal.

She scanned the counters. "Do you want to eat here or in the living room?"

"Here is fine."

"I'd like to start going over everything right now. Some of these places might be open, and we can call today to get stuff canceled. I think some of them will give back at least part of your deposits if they can rebook for the same day, so we should start calling right away."

"I guess."

"Did you keep all your receipts? Business cards with contact information?"

He pulled an envelope out from a drawer and laid it on the table. "It's all in here."

Before she finished her first piece of pizza, Tasha dumped the contents onto the table and put everything into little piles. "I don't see the bill for the cake."

"Pastor's wife is, or was, making the cake. She said she'd let me know how much it was after the wedding. She didn't want a deposit since everything was from her kitchen, anyway."

Tasha raised her head and stared straight into his eyes. "You did tell Pastor about everything, didn't you?"

"I emailed him. I can't talk to him yet. I'm too afraid he's going to try to convince me to forgive and forget, and marry her, anyway. I won't do that."

Her eyes softened, and she reached to touch the top of his hand. "The Bible doesn't actually say to forget. God just says to forgive. I don't believe God would tell us to continue in a bad situation and be hurt again, unless we want to take that risk. God tells us to forgive, which means to deal with it, then move forward, which doesn't mean to forget, just to handle it with compassion, then get on with your life without letting it eat away at you. Does that take some of the pressure off?"

All he could do was stare down at her hand, still on top of his. Her touch was gentle, and her hand was so nice and warm.

He looked up at Tasha. He hadn't thought about forgiving Heather. Truthfully, he hadn't got that far yet. So far all he felt was hurt, and stupid for not seeing what was apparently right under his nose. He was still mostly numb. Even though he hadn't seen Heather for over two days, he wasn't sure the reality of it had set in yet. But as he shifted his attention to the pile of bills and receipts on the table, he was sure that by the end of the night his head would catch up with his heart.

"Yeah," he muttered, then looked into her eyes. "That does take the pressure off."

"Do you want to talk about it?"

Until now he hadn't wanted to, even though he knew he would have to. But he wasn't sure Tasha was the best person; after all, she was Heather's sister and they lived together. He opened his mouth to say so, but the wrong words came out. "Yeah. I do."

When she gave his hand a gentle squeeze, the words began to tumble out of his mouth. "Since I was the best man, I needed to be there early, with the rest of the wedding party. You know how she takes so long to get ready. I thought if I got there really early, I could motivate her to be ready, so we could leave early.

"That woman who watches the door from her balcony on the third floor let me in when Heather didn't answer. I guess you'd already gone. When I got to your floor I saw a couple lip-locked in front of your neighbor's door. I started to go around them, then..." He gulped and squeezed his eyes shut as the picture of what he'd interrupted burst into his mind's eye like a picture in a big-screen movie theater.

Tasha's voice broke into his thoughts. "You saw it was Heather and Zac."

He nodded, then opened his eyes, preferring to see Tasha than to keep replaying what he'd stumbled onto. "I couldn't see their faces but I saw my ring on her finger. You know what went through my mind when they pulled apart? First, I stood there in shock, thinking that she'd never kissed me like that. Then I started wondering if he ever kissed his wife like that. Then it started to sink in that she was fooling around on me with a married man. You know what she said to me? That it wasn't what it looked like."

He covered his eyes with his free hand, as if he could make the image go away. "And that made me look harder. She was carrying her shoes, and her buttons were done up wrong." As the image kept repeating in his head, he didn't know what he felt like doing worse, screaming or putting his fist through the wall. "It wasn't what it looked like. It was worse."

Tasha gasped, and her grip around his fingers tightened.

He lowered his hand from his face and stared into Tasha's eyes, wide with shock. "Before I did something I would regret, I demanded my ring back and walked away. I couldn't go to Luis's wedding in that frame of mind, so I went down into the exercise room and beat on the punching bag for a while to get it out of my system, then went to the wedding." He gulped. "It was really hard."

As he continued to stare into Tasha's eyes, they became glassy.

She quickly released his hand. Strangely, he suddenly felt really cold.

Tasha turned around, swiped her sleeve across her eyes, sniffled, then sucked in a deep breath. "I'm so sorry. I don't know what to say."

For lack of something better to do, he pushed away the pizza box, and straightened the pile of bills. "There's nothing to say. It's over. Now let's start canceling everything. The sooner it's all done, the better."

Tasha swiped her sleeve over her eyes once more, then picked up her phone, and started dialing the number on the bill that was on top of the pile, which was the caterer. "This will be the most expensive," she muttered, then cleared her throat while waiting for someone to answer.

He thought she was going to get voice mail, but she got a real person. Talking to the man, she switched gears like flicking a switch. In the blink of an eye, she was all business. She was polite and asked nicely rather than demanded if it was possible to get at least a partial refund for the cancellation. She nodded a few times, thanked the person and hung up.

"That sounds promising. He says they double booked that weekend, but he's having trouble finding staff for the second commitment. He was almost relieved to have a cancellation. His only consideration will be to confirm that he hasn't already ordered the ingredients and all the meat from his supplier. If not, he'll give you back most of your deposit. He said he'd call tomorrow and let you know. What's next?"

"I guess the hall, and then the decorating place. I already canceled the tux rental when they called this afternoon to get an appointment for a fitting. They wouldn't give me back the deposit, though."

"What about music? Did you hire a DJ?"

"Yes, but it's someone I know. He didn't ask for a deposit. If he can't rebook I'm going to send him something because it's the right thing to do. But since he gave me a big discount for being a friend, if he rebooks he's going to make more money than what I was going to pay him, so he'll be ahead. I'll text him right now."

"Then I'll call the hotel."

While he texted his friend, he listened to Tasha. Even though the person she needed to speak to was gone for the day, the person answering said that they could probably get half of the deposit back if they could rebook that day, which was very likely because they always had a waiting list.

Unfortunately, everything else was closed for the

day, but Tasha left voice mails and helped him write emails to follow them all up.

"That's done, as much as we can do. But everyone's been notified. We'll just have to see what happens and what you can get back."

It hadn't been as painful as he thought it would be. Although the hardest part was going to be telling his friends and relatives the wedding was off.

It had been easy telling the guys at work. They weren't really his friends, and he hadn't invited them to the wedding. So far only a few of his real friends knew, and none of his family.

He didn't know how to tell them. His mother had told him his wedding was going to be the second best thing that had happened in her life, the first being his birth. He didn't really believe that, but he wasn't going to contradict her.

Still, he had no doubt in his mind. Telling his mother the wedding was canceled was going to be the hardest thing he ever had to do.

Texting would be easier than a face-to-face conversation, but he couldn't do that to her.

She was going to cry. He knew it. The last thing he wanted to do was make his mother cry. First, she'd cry, then she'd try to be strong and suck it up; she'd empathize, and then he'd probably cry, too.

He hadn't cried since he was twelve, when the conservation officer said that the injured baby duck he'd rescued was probably going to die.

He'd saved a duck from a broken leg and a broken wing, but he couldn't save his mother from a broken heart.

"You haven't told your mother yet, have you?"

Jeff gulped. "No. How could you tell what I was thinking?"

Tasha shrugged her shoulders and made a weak smile. "Just your expression. Your face went all soft, and it looked like you were thinking of something really sad. What we've done so far may be the expensive stuff, but it was the easy part. Now you have to tell all your friends and relatives, starting with your family. You probably should tell your mother tonight. I hope she hasn't already heard it from someone else."

"You're right." He gulped again. The situation was bad enough, but worse if he wasn't the one to tell her. "She isn't going to take this well. She's going to…get all emotional and stuff. I don't want to do that to her. She was so excited about the wedding." And likely also the possibility of being a grandmother, even though she adamantly denied she was thinking about it before he was even married.

Tasha stared at his phone lying on the table between them. He almost felt her mentally poking him to pick it up.

The second he did, she stood. "I'll leave you to make this call in private. Maybe I'll see you tomorrow."

He opened his mouth to tell her to stay, that he wanted her to be there when he was done, but before he could get a word out, she was gone.

Chapter 4

Natasha stared at a blank spot on the living room wall.

Ever since she'd found out from Jeff what Heather had done, she'd known this moment would come.

Deep down, or maybe even not so deep, she'd known the right thing to do. But now that she'd had the inevitable face-to-face with Heather, she didn't know which way to turn.

From inside her purse, her cell phone sang out the theme from the *The Muppet Show*.

Instead of answering, she checked the call display. Jeff.

Last night, seeing his expression as she left, she could guess at how the conversation with his mother had gone. He probably needed a friend to talk to, but the way she was feeling after having it out with Heather, she couldn't be that friend.

She let the call go to voice mail, tucking the phone back into its pocket in her purse. Before she managed to rezip it, a tone sounded that she'd received a text message.

That, she could deal with. She pulled her phone back out. The text was from Jeff.

R U there? Can I come over?

For today, she couldn't see him—she needed to be alone with her thoughts, and her conscience. She typed out her reply.

Maybe tomorrow.

Tomorrow, after a little time, she would be able to hold herself together. But not now.

Heather would be back in about an hour, and before that happened she needed to calm down.

A cup of herbal tea was a good place to start.

While she waited for the kettle to boil she changed into her most comfortable sweatpants and T-shirt, not caring that she had a stain on the shirt and a hole in her left knee. As she poured the boiled water into the teapot, the buzzer for the door sounded.

Natasha checked the time. Right on schedule, her upstairs neighbor's son's friend had arrived to play online games. He always brought his laptop computer, a bag of fast food and a large drink, and rather than put something down, he often buzzed the wrong suite. She pushed the button to answer. "You hit the wrong button again, Brad."

"It's not Brad. It's me. Jeff. Can I come in?"

Natasha's finger froze. Instead of the button to open the door, she pressed the button to speak again. "What are you doing here?"

"I was in the neighborhood and had a doughnut craving, so I brought some to share."

The time between the phone call she never answered and his arrival was exactly the amount of time it took to drive from his house to her apartment.

"If you don't let me in, I can always ask that nice lady on the third floor, who is already waving at me from her balcony."

Natasha didn't know the woman's name, but a major part of the woman's day seemed to be checking who came in and out. She knew many of the tenants' friends and relatives by face, if not by name, and often let people in when she probably shouldn't have. Most people appreciated her because she also let in tenants when they had their hands full and would have struggled with the key.

She never let Brad in, but she would let Jeff in. Natasha hit the button to open the door.

She looked down at her ratty clothes, and wiggled her bare toes. She didn't have time to change, but she did have time to splash some cold water on her face and put on some socks.

Jeff's knock echoed on the door just as she closed her dresser drawer.

When she opened the door he didn't wait for an invitation, but walked straight in holding two take-out cups of coffee and a paper bag.

He continued into the kitchen, so she followed him. He set both cups on the table, and sat, making himself quite at home. "You sounded sad, so I thought I'd come over and keep you company."

"We never spoke."

He shrugged his shoulders. "Your text sounded sad."

All she could do was glare at him.

Jeff sighed. "You probably talked to Heather when you got home from work, didn't you?"

"Yes." It was the first time they'd actually spoken since Jeff told her what her sister was doing, and with whom. It hadn't been pleasant.

He eyed her up and down. Hopefully her eyes weren't as puffy as they'd been.

He turned to the teapot on the counter. "Looks like you've got your choice of beverages. If you want tea, I'll drink both cups of coffee." He turned back to her. "My last conversation with Heather wasn't so great, but that was the end. That can't happen for you. Not only is she your sister, you also live with her. I feel like I'm sticking you in the middle of everything, and you shouldn't be there." He opened the bag and pushed it toward her. "I probably should tell you that it's my problem, not yours, and you should just carry on with your sister like you always have, but I know it's not that simple. You have to live with her, and…what she's doing is wrong."

Natasha thought she'd managed to get her sniffles under control, but her eyes started to burn again. "You know that old standby to love the sinner but hate the sin. In so many ways it sounds so flippant, but when it comes down to the bottom line, it's not so easy when it's right in your face." As if it wasn't hard enough to deal with someone who was doing something so wrong as cheating on her fiancé with a married man, Natasha also had been in love with that now-ex-fiancé for a long time. His hurt was her hurt, made worse that her own sister was the one doing the hurting. If that weren't bad enough, Natasha couldn't push away the guilt at being in love with him in the first place, when he really hadn't been hers to love. Unlike her sister, though, she hadn't acted on pursuing a man who wasn't free to start a relationship.

Now he was single, but she didn't know what to do in the face of Heather's accusations.

He looked at her in such a way that she couldn't read his expression. Before she could try to analyze it he stood, walked to the cupboard and opened it, staring at the mugs as if trying to decide which to select. When he spoke he didn't turn around, but remained with his back to her. "I'm probably torturing myself, but I need to hear what she said. Is she sorry for what she's done?"

Pain coursed through her, but the best option was the truth. After all, lies were the root of the problem. The word *sorry* hadn't entered the conversation, even once.

"The first thing she said was that she didn't mean to cheat on you. She said she was just being neighborly with Zac, that they were just friends. But then it became more, and one night when his wife was away things got out of hand."

Jeff snorted, still not turning around. "She didn't mean it? They were sneaking around to see each other. You're her sister—you live with her—and you didn't even know." He spun around. "And what does she mean by things getting out of hand? We were four weeks away from getting married! If she felt herself falling for another guy, she should have either split up with me, or stopped seeing him—not snuck around to see him behind my back." He raised one hand, waving it in the air. "And he's married! He should have been out of bounds!"

He paused, his chest heaving. "Sorry. I didn't mean to yell. This isn't your fault."

Heather had accused her of exactly the opposite, that it was, in fact, all Natasha's fault. That she should have seen it, and told Heather to stop. Except that she couldn't see what she didn't know. "It's okay. I know you're upset."

He waited as he calmed a bit, then spoke with his voice lowered. "Remember that little song we learned in Sunday school when we were kids, about fleeing from temptation? It's even more applicable to adults. If I was spending time with a woman who tempted me, I would step away and not see her again, and get myself out of the line of fire."

Natasha's heart sank even more. She didn't tempt him. At all. If she did, he would have walked away, and he certainly hadn't done that. Over the past year she'd spent a lot of time with him, and that's how she'd fallen in love with him.

She cleared her throat and stiffened in an attempt to give herself strength. "She said that you weren't paying enough attention to her. Zac needed her, and you didn't, and that's why it happened."

"What?" His breathing quickened, and his fists clenched.

While silence hung in the air, more of Heather's words pierced her. Heather had accused Natasha of being unforgiving and encouraging Jeff to break up instead of reconciling. She'd said that, as sisters, Natasha should have been on her side and helped her to make things right, not to destroy her happiness.

Her words were partially true. While she hadn't actually encouraged Jeff to break up, she had told him that it was okay that he did, that he wasn't obligated to resume the relationship as if nothing had happened. If that hadn't made her feel guilty enough, deep down she really didn't want Jeff to marry Heather, not just because she didn't think Heather and Jeff were suited. She couldn't bear the thought of someone she loved, even though he would never love her back, being hurt by a cheating spouse, who happened to be her sister. Although obviously Jeff had loved her sister, and not her. Maybe he still did. She didn't know, and she was too afraid to ask.

Jeff looked at the clock on the stove, and stood. "I know she's going to be home in a few minutes. If I see her I'm going to say something I'll later regret. I think we should go. Besides, I think you need a change of scenery."

Before she could question his use of the word *we*, he took her wrist and led her to the door.

"I don't want to see her, either, but I'm a mess. I can't go anywhere looking like this."

He eyed her up and down, only pausing for a second at the hole in her knee. "I go places with holes in my jeans all the time. But if it bugs you we'll go someplace where no one will see you."

"Wait. I need my purse."

She ran to the kitchen, grabbed her purse, then hurried back to the door, where Jeff stood with his arms crossed. She slipped her feet into her sneakers, and once they were in the hall, he stopped only long enough for her to lock the door, then ran down the hall, still holding her wrist, to the elevator, and hit the button. It opened within seconds.

Fortunately, no one was in the lobby when the door opened. He once again grabbed her wrist, and they rushed out to his car.

Before she could ask where they were going, he put the car into Reverse, ready to back up.

Heather's car came around the corner, then turned to the entrance for the underground parking.

Instead of watching her sister, she turned to Jeff. He gritted his teeth and clenched the steering wheel in a death grip. "I know the perfect place. Buckle up."

* * *

Jeff grasped the steering wheel tighter to stop his hands from shaking.

When he'd gotten out of the elevator on Tasha's floor and looked down the hall, he'd had a flashback of the moment he'd seen Heather locked in the arms of the other man.

Not only was she not sorry, now she'd upset Tasha.

He didn't know why he'd dragged Tasha with him, except that he didn't want to be alone. Or maybe it was because after what happened, even though he didn't know all the details, he didn't want Tasha to be alone, either.

What a pair they made.

One day, they'd be able to look back and analyze the decisions they'd made. But for now, he knew he wasn't thinking all that rationally. He'd dragged her out of her home when she obviously wasn't prepared to be seen in public. He would have to make it up to her.

He turned to her and tried to smile, but knew it looked as lame as it felt. "I think I left the doughnuts on your table. Are you hungry?"

She shook her head. "No."

"Did you eat supper?"

She shook her head again, and pressed her hands to her stomach. "No."

Then he needed to find her some comfort food, except he didn't know anywhere that served bacon on a take-out basis at suppertime. "I promised I knew the perfect place to go, but it would be more perfect if we brought something to eat. How about if I pick up a couple of burgers, and we'll have something better another time."

Her hands remained pressed to her stomach. "I'm really not hungry."

"I am, and I don't want to eat alone."

He headed for the nearest burger place that had a drive-through window. Once the bag of warm food was in the car, her stomach grumbled, which confirmed his suspicion. He drove quickly to the park and pulled into a spot at the far end of the lot, away from the other cars.

She looked around them, but didn't get out of the car. "What are we doing here?"

"We're going to have supper, then we're going to go for a walk. Is that okay with you?"

She looked out the window. "We were just here a few days ago." She turned back to him. "Are we here because you're hoping to see more ducks?"

"We won't see any now—it will be dark in less than an hour. But it's a nice walk, and I think we both need it."

She turned toward the sun, which was already golden and nearly touching the horizon. "I think even less than half an hour. It's getting cold in the evenings. I wonder if we're going to need jackets?"

He hadn't brought a jacket because when he left home he'd only thought of going from the car to the building. Likewise, all Tasha had was a T-shirt, leaving her arms bare. People already on the path all wore jackets. "Maybe this wasn't such a good idea, after all."

She turned to him and rested one hand on his arm. "It's okay. How about if we eat in the car, then instead of going for a walk we can just jog to the lake, look for some ducks and jog back."

"Sure."

They ate in silence, which was fine with Jeff. He didn't know what to say, anyway.

Tasha sighed. "The sunset sure is pretty, isn't it?"

"Yeah." Sitting in the car at the almost-deserted park watching the sunset made him think of high school, how the guys would bring a girl here hoping for a romantic moment, which hadn't ever happened to him. Of course, now he knew what to do to make such a moment romantic, but he was with Tasha.

It was getting a little chilly, and he wished he'd bought two coffees instead of iced soft drinks. He was about to ask if she wanted to just forget it and go home when she stuffed her empty wrappers in the bag and started digging through her purse. "What are you doing?"

"Getting my camera. That sunset is really pretty. I think the prettiest sunsets are in the fall, don't you?"

"I guess. I've never really thought about it."

"I'm ready, let's go."

The second the doors opened, a cold draft blew through the car. "Wait. I just thought of something. I need to get something out of the trunk."

She didn't wait. While he went to the rear of the car, Tasha jogged to the shore of the lake. As soon as he got what he wanted, he joined her.

"Hold still," he said, then stepped close beside her and tossed the blanket around their shoulders.

"How did you get this?"

"I always keep a blanket and a bag of kitty litter in the trunk. Just in case."

She turned to him. "In case of what? You think you're going to find a cat in distress from holding it too long?"

Jeff shook his head. "No. If it snows and you get stuck, you put cat litter in front of the drive tires to provide a little traction, and you can get out."

"Really?"

"That's what I read. It's never happened to me, but if it does, I'm ready. That's also why I have the blanket. It's part of my emergency kit."

Tasha giggled, which he thought was a good thing. "This isn't an emergency. But the blanket is probably a good idea."

As he steadied the half of the blanket on her shoulder, Tasha raised her camera and started taking her pictures. When she lowered the camera to check her shot he flipped the blanket so his arm was under it, then grasping a handful of it, he put his arm over her shoulders and held the corner under her chin to cover her more completely. To get maximum warmth, he shuffled so they were pressed together side by side, and pulled the blanket more securely around both of them.

Tasha stiffened. "What are you doing?"

"Keeping us warm. It's cold with the breeze coming over the lake." The blanket felt comfortably warm, and good. But not only the blanket… He liked having Tasha snuggled in beside him, his arm around her shoulders. It somehow felt…right.

"I guess you're right. Just before you came with the blanket my teeth were starting to chatter." She raised the camera and moved it around in front of her to compose her shot.

He raised his left hand, with his side of the blanket still grasped in his fist, and pointed to one of the tall trees. "That would make a good shot. See how the red of the sunset is peeking through the branches?"

"Yeah. That looks good." She turned and snapped a few shots, then turned back to the way she'd been facing before.

Jeff simply watched. He hadn't taken the time to just relax and take photos for a long time. It was something he'd always enjoyed, and he didn't know when, or why, he'd stopped. Although mostly, he suspected it was simply because Heather didn't like to take walks in the park, especially along the dusty path. As time went on, instead of walking on the trails, they'd done their walking on the concrete, window-shopping. He didn't mind window-shopping, but now that he was at the park, it was no contest; he liked walking along the trail more.

Almost as if he needed to prove a point, Jeff motioned to the left with his head. "I think we'd be warmer if we walked a bit. Want to?"

Tasha paused for a few seconds, then shrugged her shoulders, turned off her camera and slipped it into her pocket. "I don't see why not. The sun is almost down, but we still have a few minutes."

He almost asked if she wanted him to bring the blanket back to the car, but then thought of how nice it felt to be sharing their body heat against the breeze off the lake.

As he turned she looked at him with raised eyebrows. All he did was smile at her and give her shoulder a little squeeze. She capitulated by allowing him to guide their turn toward the trail, then walked with him, tucked in the blanket, along the shoreline.

All Jeff could think of was how relaxed he felt as they ventured slowly alongside the water's edge. How right this was, and how much he needed this break. He hoped she felt the same, but he didn't know how to put his thoughts into words.

Beside him, Tasha sighed. "This was a really good idea. Getting away from it all. Thanks."

"No worries. But we need to turn around. I brought my blanket, but I didn't bring my emergency flashlight. I don't want us to trip on the uneven ground on the way back to the car."

He felt the movement of Tasha wiggling under the blanket. One hand stuck out from beneath the blanket, holding her cell phone. She pushed the button and looked at the screen. "I have lots of battery left. This is *my* emergency flashlight."

He grinned at her ingenuity, and they kept going in silence.

They walked until they couldn't make out any detail in the gravel path, then stopped to look at the lake, shimmering in the last feeble glimmers of light.

He'd thought it was good before, but now, he didn't want the moment to end. The only thing that would have made the night better would have been if the sky was clear, so they could see the stars.

Light flashed from Tasha's phone, cutting through the blackness at their feet. "It's time to go back. We both have to get up for work in the morning."

He really *didn't* want the moment to end, and that made no sense. He needed to be up at 5:30 a.m.

Whatever was going on in his head, he'd figure it out tomorrow.

Chapter 5

Natasha sat on the couch trying to watch television, but found it difficult to concentrate, even though her favorite show was on.

Four weeks had gone by quickly.

Once more Heather interrupted her, this time running in front of her on the way to the closet. Heather dropped to her knees, and began digging through the pile of shoes.

"Have you seen my red sandals? The ones with the gold straps."

Natasha sighed, hit the pause button on the DVR and turned to her sister. "Didn't you pack up all your summer shoes and put them in that box on the shelf? The one marked Summer Shoes?"

"Right. I forgot. Thanks." Heather stood, stretched, grabbed the box and pulled it down.

Natasha crossed her arms and stared at her sister. "Why are you in such a panic to pack now? You're not leaving until tomorrow night."

Tomorrow. The day of the wedding that wasn't.

Heather's voice turned whiny. "I don't want to leave it until the last minute, in case I have to go shopping to get something I forgot. Although I may go shopping, anyway. I need to take a break to get away from all the stress."

Natasha bit her tongue. She almost said that Heather was the cause of her own stress, but wanted to avoid another argument. It had been three weeks since they'd had a confrontation, and as far as she knew, Heather wasn't seeing their neighbor anymore. But then, Natasha hadn't known Heather had been seeing him in the first place.

Four weeks after Jeff ended their engagement, Heather seemed to have no trouble getting on with her life. She was still going to use the honeymoon package, but now as a vacation with a friend she worked with.

Jeff had been making good progress and moving forward, although there were times she could tell he was still thinking about it. He'd obviously been more in love with Heather than Heather had been with him.

Together Natasha and Jeff had joined the Bible study meeting that met every Thursday evening at her friend Ashley's church. He'd told everyone there the short version of what happened. Last meeting he'd been sullen, and then when someone asked him what was wrong, he'd gone silent. Earlier that night, Luis had taken Jeff on a trip to Portland to see a Blazers game—something she didn't understand because Jeff didn't particularly like basketball. But the trip would serve the purpose of keeping Jeff's mind occupied, since Luis made a point of taking Jeff's car so that Jeff would drive.

She smiled. Luis would probably have made Jeff pay for the gas, as well as the parking. But Luis wanted what was best for Jeff, as these past few days had been particularly difficult for him.

Tomorrow, the day he was supposed to get married, was going to be the most difficult of all. All his friends agreed that she would be the best person to keep him busy for the day, since he seemed better when he was with her. So, for Saturday, she'd planned a day in the park, taking pictures and looking for ducks. However, the forecast was for colder temperatures and heavy rain, which would be fine for ducks, but not very fine for people.

The blanket he had in the trunk was great for cold, but not so good for wet.

"I found them!" Heather sang out, holding up her red sandals, as if Natasha cared. "Now I can pack my red shorts." Heather dashed back to the bedroom, followed by the slamming of drawers.

As Natasha reached to turn up the volume on the television, her phone sang the tune for receiving a text message.

It was from Jeff.

I M bored. I hate basketball. Wish U wr here.

She couldn't help but smile as she replied.

Why, so we cud hate it together?

She waited for his reply, knowing he couldn't type as fast as she could with his large thumbs.

Yes. Then it wudnt be so bad.

She hit the prompt to reply but her thumbs wouldn't work to type a message. Even though she didn't like basketball, either, she did wish she were with him. But it would be ridiculous for both of them to sit there and watch a sport neither of them enjoyed. Therefore it was best to change the subject.

Maybe a hot dog wud make it better.

Food seemed to make a lot of things better for Jeff. Since the breakup he'd gained a few pounds, and so had she. She didn't know if it was good or bad to discover he liked to cook dinner for her, and on the weekends brunch, as well. While many women comforted themselves with chocolate and ice cream, she found out the hard way that Jeff's comfort food was bacon. On everything.

Luis went to get some dogs. Gotta go. Here he comes.

She couldn't help but smile imagining Luis's response to catching Jeff texting when he should have been watching the game. Luis had told her how much he'd spent on the tickets, and they weren't cheap.

She almost asked if stadium hot dogs had bacon on them, but didn't want to get him in worse trouble with his friend.

The phone was barely back in her purse when the text ringtone sang out again.

Now she really did smile, imagining Luis scolding Jeff, and Jeff texting her to tell her all about it, while Luis was watching.

Her smile dropped when she saw the sender. It wasn't Jeff. It wasn't even Luis. It was her boss.

Bill never texted her unless it was something critical he didn't want to say in person.

Worse, it was Friday night. After hours. And she knew this wasn't a social call. As the HR director, it could only be something bad.

Her hand trembled as she hit the prompt to read the message.

It was long. That meant it was really bad.

Sorry to text. Due to a family emergency Gloria and I must leave tonight for about a month. I need you to organize and do all the shopping for the Christmas party this year. I have emailed you the files. I know you will use personal time. I will give you a good bonus. Thank you.

Visions danced in her head. Not of sugarplums,

but visions of all she had to do. At the stationery store where she worked, the company Christmas party was for all employees, both office and sales staff, their spouses or significant others, and their children. Last year there had been approximately twenty children at the party, and the company had purchased a gift for every one of them. This year they'd expanded their staff, which meant…more children at the party.

Bill's wife, who didn't work, always did all the shopping and wrapping, plus she organized the catering. Every year she made a point that their company wouldn't do the same as when she was a little girl—every girl got a doll and every boy got a toy car. Gloria made sure every child received a different and personally selected gift, and not something selected by a parent. Gloria based the amount spent on a child by the child's age, with no concession made regarding a parent's seniority or performance record. It was all about the kids.

Natasha flipped to the calendar app in her phone. She'd already marked the day of the party, which was just over a week before Christmas.

Until now, she hadn't entertained any thoughts of Christmas, though many stores already featured Christmas trees and some decorations. While she loved the Christmas season, she usually tried to have most of her shopping done by Black Friday. But now, instead of a dozen gifts, she needed to buy about fifty more. Most of them for children of people she barely knew.

Natasha looked outside to the black night. With the

sound of an electronic version of the Muppets theme, everything had changed.

Now she wouldn't be taking Jeff to the park. She had another activity to keep him busy.

Whether he liked it or not.

Jeff turned off the alarm, then pulled the blanket over his head.

After the game Luis had taken him out for a burger, then they'd endured the three-hour drive home.

He didn't want to get up. The greasy burger still sat like a lump in his stomach.

More than that, what really sat like a lump in his stomach was the fact that today would have been the day he was getting married.

This was a day to spend in bed. Or maybe he'd just sit on the couch in his pajamas and not move except to eat. That was what single guys did on a rainy fall morning when they were all alone and wanted to stay that way. He'd even watch another basketball game, if that's all he could find on television.

Or he could man-up and spend the day with…the sister of the woman who'd been cheating on him.

He turned to bury his face in the pillow. He didn't know why he'd agreed to spend the day with Tasha. Especially today. Being with someone who looked so much like the woman who'd stomped on his heart would be like rubbing a dog's nose in an accident.

But that's exactly what it had been. An accident. Since he broke off the engagement he'd spent most of his nonworking time with Tasha. At first he thought she was only being nice, capitulating and doing things with him that he wanted to do. In the same way, because she was so accommodating to him when he was down, he agreed to do what she wanted before he even knew what it was—as they took turns choosing what they would be doing.

He didn't know when they started picking the same things, or even more strange, when saying goodbye at the end of an evening, he couldn't remember who suggested their activity of the day.

Unlike his time with Heather. During the past year, everything he'd done with Heather was because he simply gave in. Heather seldom asked what he wanted. He'd learned to make the best of her choices and enjoyed himself in spite of it.

After he'd been dumped by Kate he'd wanted to get back into a relationship so badly, he'd acquiesced to Heather for all the wrong reasons.

It wasn't surprising that she'd said yes when he asked her to marry him. He'd been like an abused puppy, doing everything she wanted, when she wanted it, on her terms, and paying for it all, too. To keep him from realizing the pattern he'd fallen into, she'd treated him like a knight in shining armor so he'd felt like a hero, sacrificing what he really wanted for her.

He'd given her everything she wanted, in exchange for the pleasure of her company.

Now that his eyes were open, he would never allow himself to fall for it again.

From now on, any relationship would be on his terms.

And today, his terms were that he was going to celebrate his freedom by spending the whole day alone, in whatever state he wanted.

He was going to stay in bed until noon, and nothing was going to change that.

From the table beside the bed, his cell phone rang out with the tune of the Mario Kart theme, which meant it was Tasha.

He'd already answered before he remembered that he promised himself he was going to spend the day alone. But he could justify answering her call by telling himself that his mother had raised him to have manners. Since he'd previously agreed to spend the day with Tasha, he owed it to her to tell her he'd changed his mind, versus letting her call go to voice mail and leaving her hanging all day.

"Hi, Jeff. It's me. Natasha."

He grinned. As if he didn't already know. "Hi. Listen. About today. I—"

"I'm sorry about our plans," she blurted out before he could finish his sentence. "My boss just called with a big assignment."

He felt his grin drop. Even though he was going to cancel, he didn't want to see her work through the weekend. She worked hard all week, even through her breaks so she could get off on time to be with him. She deserved her free time. "Is there anything I can do?" he asked before he thought about his promise to himself to spend the day alone on the couch.

"I'm so glad you asked. I need your help."

"Sure. Name it." The words were out and then he

thought of what he was obligating himself to. Before he said any more, he gritted his teeth, trying to think of how he could backtrack his offer.

"I need to go shopping."

At her words, his mouth opened, ready to decline. He hated shopping.

She continued before he could respond. "Christmas shopping."

For that, he could respond. "Seriously? Count me..." The word *out* hung on his lips, but he couldn't say it. It wasn't realistic, but it was as if he could feel her disappointment if he said what he really thought.

He didn't just hate Christmas shopping. He detested it. But Tasha had come through to help him when he was down. He didn't know why she needed his help, unless she was buying something really heavy. Or she needed something that wouldn't fit into her little car.

He sighed. "...in. Count me in." He looked down and wiggled his bare toes. "I just need to get dressed, and I'll be right over."

After they said their goodbyes, he got in and out of the shower and dressed in record time. He didn't want to think of why he would ever be in a hurry to go shopping, especially with a woman. As he drove in the rain to her building, by the time he turned the corner to get to her block, he wondered why he wasn't as worried about his behavior as he should have been.

When he pulled into the visitor parking, Tasha was waiting.

She hopped in, buckled her seat belt and turned to

him. "Let's go." She swiped some rain off her cheeks, then started fiddling with her purse.

He almost asked why she had come down to wait for him, but then he realized that Heather was likely still in the apartment.

Tasha had waited for him outside, in the rain, so he wouldn't have to see Heather.

He gulped. He would make this up to her. He didn't know how, but he would. "Where to?"

As he reversed the car, she pulled her computer tablet out of her purse, tapped it a few times, then started reading. "I think we should do the easy ones first, so let's go to that big store that sells baby stuff."

"Who do you know that has a baby?" He tried to think of her friends he'd met in the past few weeks. At the most likely prospect, his stomach clenched. "Your friend who just got married. Ashley. Is she pregnant?" He was nearing thirty, and he wanted to start a family not too long after getting married. If her friend was pregnant already, of course he was happy for Ashley and Dave, but it also smacked him in the face, reminding him of something else that had been yanked from him.

Beside him, Tasha shook her head as she tapped something into her tablet. "No, not yet, but I'm sure it won't be long. I've got to buy four baby gifts for my list. Two girls and one boy. And one unknown, because the baby is due next week."

"How many friends with babies do you have?"

She looked up at him. "These aren't for my friends. These are for coworkers' children. This is what my boss needs me to do." She explained about the text she'd received.

"I feel like I should be afraid to ask why you feel you need my help. You know I hate shopping."

"I know. But half my list is boys, and I have no idea what to buy for boys."

He grinned. "Cars," he said with no hesitation. "The faster, the better."

"I can't. It's company policy for no two children to receive the same thing. It would be easy if I could buy typical boy and girl gifts and divide them up, but I can't. The reason this is so special is that no two children get the same gift."

Since the light was red, when Jeff came to a complete stop he turned to Tasha. By now she was reading on the tablet, and from that angle he couldn't see it. "I thought for all these company parties the parents bought the gifts and snuck them under the tree for Santa to hand out."

She shook her head. "That's not the way my boss does it. It's as big a surprise for the parents as it is for the kids." She held up the tablet again. "He's also got a scale of how much to spend. It's all based on the age of the kids, not what position the parent holds, or how long they've been working there. He's a really great boss."

Mentally he mapped out his route, and turned the corner. "I don't understand why he gave you this job."

"Because I'm the human resources director. Although I only handle adults. I don't know what to do with children. Especially boys."

Rather than look at her, he focused all his attention to the traffic ahead of him. She didn't know how to handle boys, but she sure knew how to handle men. Especially him. She'd done everything right to lift him out of the hole he'd fallen into, and it hadn't occurred to him that she was a professional at handling people. But as HR director, that was her job.

And now that she'd mentioned it, when her newly married friend Ashley, who he now saw every week at the Bible study meeting, had been shot in a bank robbery, Tasha had gone to a monthlong workshop for human resources directors.

Her natural talents were probably enhanced by everything she'd learned for use in the workplace. She knew exactly what he needed when his life blew up in his face.

He wasn't sure how to feel about his realization that he'd been her subject to test her new skills, but the timing worked for both of them. In only a month he felt pretty much back to normal and ready to get on with his life.

So, the first thing he was going to do was to return the favor.

Besides, it might be fun. He didn't like shopping but he could appreciate toys, and Tasha was a Christmas junkie.

He pulled into the parking lot, and gave her a big smile. "I'm all yours. Lead the way."

Chapter 6

Natasha stood beside Jeff as he once more repositioned the boxes in the trunk of the car, stepped back to judge the height and carefully pushed the trunk closed.

She tried not to cringe as the latch engaged, knowing he was watching her out of the corner of his eye.

He slapped his hands together. "See? I told you I could make everything fit." He turned toward her, grinning ear to ear.

Her breath caught. A flock of butterflies went to war in her stomach, even though butterflies were well out of season right now. If only he would smile like that more often.

No, she didn't want him to smile like that. When he did her brain short-circuited, and she needed her brain to be working at peak efficiency right now. She had too much to do—she couldn't allow herself to be distracted.

His grin widened. "I saw your expression. You didn't think I could do it." His grin dropped as he turned back toward the store. "I almost didn't, though. I don't understand how baby stuff takes up so much room."

She hiked her purse strap over her shoulder, then turned to reach for the car's door handle. "Because baby stuff is made from big pieces." Since all three of the babies were under nine months old, and one wasn't even born yet, she'd been pretty safe to guess none of them were walking. "My boss said to buy toys, not child-care items. Stuff like diapers and clothes are mostly for the parents. He only wants to give toys and fun stuff, so that's what I've got to do. I think so far so good. We bought some nice big, bright stuff that babies will enjoy."

Interestingly, Jeff had seemed fascinated with much of the baby paraphernalia. She'd thought at first it was because he'd never been in a store that sold products exclusively for babies, but there was something more, and she couldn't put her finger on it.

"I hope you've got batteries on your list," he said. "That's how all this stuff moves and lights up, you know."

"Of course I know. Now let's get home and get unloaded so we can make a second trip before everything closes."

"What do you mean, second trip? Just how many toys do we need to buy today?"

"We have more to shop for than we can buy in one day." Natasha gulped and tried to look cheerful when she dropped the bomb on him. "Four down, forty-six to go."

Jeff froze. "Excuse me? Did I hear you right? That means you have to buy fifty Christmas presents?"

"I told you, I have to buy a toy for every child under eighteen of every employee."

"Wow." He ran his fingers through his hair. "When I saw the list on your tablet, I didn't know it scrolled to more pages."

"Yes. Multiple pages."

"I hope you're being adequately compensated for this."

"Yes. I'm not getting money, but he's giving me an extra week of paid vacation." Not as if she had anywhere to go on that vacation, but at least she'd be able to put her feet up and relax in the comfort of her own home. When Heather wasn't there. Come to think of it, she really didn't want the extra time off with nowhere to go.

Jeff turned toward the driver's door and opened it, speaking to her as they both seated themselves and fastened their seat belts. "I can't believe all we bought was four things and the car is full."

Natasha turned around to look at the two boxes that filled the entire back of Jeff's car. Mentally she calculated how much wrapping paper she would need just for the four gifts they'd bought today. "I think that's because everything we bought today is mostly assembled and all large pieces. Plus everything is surrounded with Styrofoam." Natasha bit back a grin, remembering his frustration that they had to move the car to open the door wide enough to fit the large box now in the backseat, and he'd barely closed the trunk.

"That must be it. If we'd bought one more thing, one of us would have had to walk home." He turned to her and grinned. "And it's my car."

"If that happened, then you'd walk, and you'd let me drive your car home."

He opened his mouth, but no words came out, as if he were picturing himself taking the bus home.

She checked her watch. "We still have lots to buy, so we need to get moving. After we get the car emptied we'll grab a quick burger and go to the mall. Next on my list is the preschoolers."

"Oh. The mall..." His voice trailed off as he started the motor.

She turned toward him. She knew Jeff better than he thought she did, and one thing she knew without a doubt—he hated the mall. Not that he didn't like shopping. He had a basement full of tools she didn't think he'd used more than once, but most of that he got at Home Depot. "We have to go to the mall. We'll be able to buy more things. We need to organize. I think it's more efficient to buy everything on the list from youngest to oldest." At his sullen expression, she rested one hand on his forearm. "I could really use your help in picking out gifts for the boys."

"I don't know how much help I'm going to be with

this. I said I'd help, and I will. But I really don't remember what I liked to play with back then. I can remember some things around kindergarten, but not much before that."

Natasha stilled. "It can't be that hard. The preschool kids are probably easy to please. I can't imagine the toys at that age are all that gender specific. For the teen boys, probably handheld games and electronics. It will be fun buying for the teen girls. But I have no idea what to buy for the preteen boys on my list. That's what I need you for."

He turned to her as they stopped for a red light. "That's easy. If you were going to buy something for me, what would you buy?"

Natasha stared into his dreamy blue-gray eyes.

She would buy him a durable coffee mug with a lid that was obvious it came from a woman. Using it would tell everyone that he was taken.

Except all they were ever going to be was friends. He hadn't actually said that, but she more than got the message when they'd talked about fleeing temptation. He saw no need to flee from her—just the opposite. They'd seen a lot of each other when he was engaged to marry someone else, and he thought nothing of it, so she obviously didn't tempt him. It wasn't what she wanted, but to not have him as a friend would be even worse than not seeing him at all.

She cleared her throat. "I'd buy you a model car that was the same make and model of your real car." Like most guys, his car was his pride and joy. He'd bought it new, so he'd had his choice of colors and all the options, which included a heated seat and a stereo that could be heard for blocks, if he turned it up.

His eyes widened. "Really? Wow. That's such a nice thought. Do you think you could find one? I'm better at welding than the little intricate stuff, but you'd help me put it together, wouldn't you?"

She shrugged. "Probably. But for now we need to stick to my list."

Jeff shook his head. "Now that I know how much stuff you need to buy, I don't think you have that much room in your apartment. I have two relatively empty bedrooms. Would you like to keep everything at my house?"

"That's a great idea. Are you sure?"

His mouth opened, but it took him a few seconds to speak. "Probably. I guess. You'd have more room to wrap stuff, too."

She wasn't sure he'd really thought through his offer, but the opportunity was too good to pass up. "That's great. I'll do that." Also, his house was closer to the mall, which meant more shopping time and less travel time. And she hadn't thought about it until now, but it would be much easier to transport everything into his house than up to her sixteenth-floor apartment. "That's great. Let's do that."

It didn't take long and they were at his house, which she now viewed from a different perspective. It wasn't a big house, but it was certainly big enough. His furniture was more functional than decorative, and mostly in neutral colors. Everything he valued, which was his television, his stereo and his laptop computer, was in the living room. A snowboard and some sports equipment were piled in the corner of one bedroom, beside the computer printer, and the other bedroom was completely empty. They piled the recent purchases in the corner of the unused bedroom, then headed to the mall.

Jeff took the last bite of his hot dog and crumpled the wrapper. Instead of stopping for a burger, he and Tasha had opted for mall hot dogs to save time. While she finished hers, he leaned back on the mall bench and watched the crowd go by. "I can't believe how many people are here. If it's bad now, what's it going to be like after Black Friday?"

Tasha tossed her wrapper into the trash bin. "I don't know. I always try to have most of my shopping done by then. Adding fifty to my shopping list is a little overwhelming for me. Let's go."

As he pushed himself up, he thought of his own Christmas shopping list. Nine. Or now eight, because Heather was officially off.

Heather.

He didn't want to think about it, but he couldn't help realizing that, right about now, he would have been getting ready to take his place at the front of the church, preparing to take his life in a new direction of responsibility.

Instead, he was at the mall. With Tasha. Looking for toys.

They didn't get very far when Tasha skidded to a halt beside one of the kiosks.

"Look! Handmade puppets! Aren't they cute?"

"I guess. But you spent a lot more money on the baby gifts you've bought so far. Shouldn't you be spending equal amounts on each kid?"

Tasha nodded. "Within reason." She pointed to a display below the puppets. "They have costumes. I can buy a puppet and a few outfits. This is perfect for a little girl."

"Clothing for a hand puppet? Are you kidding?"

She turned and rolled her eyes at him. "Kind of like clothing for a duck, who shall remain unnamed?"

His mind flashed back to visions of Daffodil in various things his mother had made. Daffodil didn't mind being treated like a dress-up doll until the third or so time his mother changed her. The memory made him smile. "That wasn't really clothing. It was just diapers, and my mom fancied them up." But the more he thought about it, Daffodil's own diapers had lacy frills. His mother had used Daffodil as a model when they took pictures for the online catalog. While a number of them looked like dresses, a bunch were made from dark colors and had pockets. Hmm. His mother had made gender-specific duck diapers. "Never mind."

She turned and smiled at the clerk, and began to select clothing…for the puppet.

After she paid for everything and tucked the receipt into her wallet, they continued on.

"Five down, forty-five to go," he muttered, trying to sound more enthusiastic about their task than he felt.

"Don't be like that. We only just started. We've

got lots of time." However, he did note that she never checked her wristwatch. Or her calendar.

Next she led him to one of the large department stores. "They have a sale on the young children's toys this weekend. This is our next stop."

It impressed him that she wanted to save money, even though it wasn't her own money she was spending.

She pulled her tablet out of her purse. "I've got a huge amount in the toddler age group." She handed it to him. "Here's the list of the boys, with their general interests beside their names."

"Okay…"

"We have five boys and six girls under the age of three. I think we need a shopping cart."

Jeff pulled a cart out of the row and they proceeded to the toy department.

There were a few lone men and a few unaccompanied women, but mostly young couples with a small child or two in a stroller browsed the toys.

He'd expected to be like that soon, a small family on an outing, not necessarily to the mall, but being together as a unit.

But that wasn't going to happen now. Instead of getting married today, here he was with…Tasha… who was currently making angry faces as she poked at her tablet while she bought toys for other people's children.

"Having trouble with something? I'm sure your tablet didn't mean it."

She sighed, lowered the tablet and stared at him.

"I'm trying to put it into a different format—a table would be good—so I can organize it better. I guess I'll do that when I get home. Let's see what we can find."

First she picked up a toy puppy that barked when she squeezed it, then a set of soft blocks. Jeff found himself getting distracted trying to figure out a cow that mooed when it was moved, then put it down before she caught him. Next he stopped at a small table with a large pile of interlocking building blocks in a well in the center. "I had a set of those when I was a kid. I wonder if they're still the same..."

Feeling no guilt at a delay in the shopping project, he abandoned the cart and approached the small table. He didn't want to crush the toddler-size chair, so he lowered himself to his knees and picked up a few blocks. Gently he pressed a few together.

He grinned up at Natasha. "They're still the same. Watch this." Of course he couldn't remember anything he'd created as a kid, but he did love to build things—he always had. Rather than build an ordinary house, he built a boat, then snapped some toy people onto it. He made a small fish that was, of course, disproportionately large compared to the boat, but every boat needed a fish. Then he needed a small plane, along with a tree. With the remaining blocks he made a small fishing shack so he had something to fly over. As he searched for the right-size window, a small hand appeared, holding the piece he needed.

"This one?"

Not taking the piece from the child's hand, he

turned to look into the face of a small boy with big brown eyes. "Can I play with the boat?" the boy asked.

"Can I have the fish, mister?" another little voice piped in.

He turned to stare into the wide eyes of the cutest little girl he'd ever seen.

"Yeah. Here." He gave his creations to the two children, and a few more appeared, helping themselves to the other things he'd made.

"Mister, can you help me?" Another child had picked up the window piece and was struggling to snap it into place in the building Jeff had half created.

Jeff sank until he was sitting on the mat, finished the shack, gave it to the little boy, then watched the children play with the things he'd made.

He couldn't believe it. Right at that moment he should have been dressed in a tuxedo and walking down the aisle with his bride. Instead, he sat on the floor, wearing jeans with a hole in the knee that he hadn't noticed when he got dressed, playing with building bricks.

"I wish I could do that," came a man's voice from above him.

Grateful for an adult to join the group, Jeff looked up into the face of a guy about the same age as himself who was keeping an eye on the little girl who had asked for the fish.

The man smiled, watching his daughter play. "All I can make is buildings. That's pretty good."

Jeff pushed himself to his feet. He wasn't sure if

he should acknowledge the compliment, considering the recommended age level of the bricks.

The man tilted his head toward Natasha, who had the cart nearly full. "Your wife is doing all the shopping without you. Looks like she's got quite a selection there."

Jeff felt his throat tighten. "Uh… She's not my wife. She's…" His voice trailed off as he tried to think of how to explain her. His now-ex-intended-wife's sister? But she was more than that. He almost said, "A friend," but knew the man thought they were shopping for their alleged children. Saying they were only friends looked as if he was downplaying their relationship, which cheapened it. But now that he thought about it, he wasn't sure what kind of relationship they had.

He ran his fingers through his hair. "It's complicated," he muttered.

The man held up one hand. "No need to explain. Not my business."

"Daddy! Look!" The man's daughter ran to him, wrapped one arm around his leg and held up the fish made of bricks. "Look what the man made. Can you make me one?"

The guy smiled. "I can try. But there are no instructions."

Jeff looked at the holder clipped to the man's belt. "Take a picture with your phone. That's what I do when there's only one set of blueprints."

"Good idea. Thanks." While the two of them walked to the table to take pictures, Jeff looked around for Tasha.

She placed one more toy in the cart, then pulled her tablet out of her purse and tapped on it.

He had to figure out exactly what kind of relationship they had.

He approached her as she slid the tablet back into her purse. "Sorry. I think I got distracted."

"No worries. I actually got a lot of ideas watching all the parents do their shopping." She smiled graciously at him. "This is it for today. I got everything I needed."

At her words, Jeff suddenly felt as if he needed something, except he didn't know what. He felt strange and unsettled, which was probably normal, considering what day it was. He'd failed at his relationship with Heather, he'd failed at defining his relationship with Tasha and now he'd failed at helping her choose toys. Instead of analyzing them, he'd been playing with them.

Tasha ignored his inability to speak, grabbed the cart and started pushing toward the cashiers. They were almost there when she stopped and selected a few packages of wrapping paper. "It was actually helpful seeing the children watch you. I saw what interested them."

Without waiting for him to respond, she continued on her way to the checkout, so he simply followed. Just as they got to the front of the store, a clerk who was about to open her cash register spotted them. Seeing the full cart, she motioned them toward her as she unhooked the chain. Jeff unloaded the cart while

Tasha dug through her purse for her wallet, then paid for everything.

Before he knew it, they were both loaded up with bags and making their way through the mall and back to his car. Even though they'd bought for far more children than their first excursion, their new purchases took less room, and they were soon on their way to his house.

The closer they got, the more and more he didn't want to just unload the car and watch Tasha leave. He didn't want to be alone, but he didn't know how to ask her to stay without looking as needy as he felt.

Beside him, she sighed. "I'm so tired after all that shopping. I really don't feel like cooking, and I'm too wiped to go out. How would you like to pick up Chinese food before we get to your place?"

"That sounds like a great idea." He reached into his pocket, and handed her his cell phone. "It's on my speed dial under Chinese."

"Why does this not surprise me?" Despite her slight sarcasm, he noticed her grinning as she hit the button and waited for them to answer.

As he drove, he watched her out of the corner of his eye. With the phone to her ear, her eyes suddenly widened. "They know you," she whispered to him "They said your name when they answered."

He smiled. "Yeah."

She cleared her throat and spoke into the phone. "This isn't Jeff, but whatever he usually orders, make it two, and he'll be there in about twenty minutes to pick it up."

For the first time all day, he actually felt like laughing. Maybe the shopping trip was exactly what he needed, after all.

When he ran into the restaurant to pay, the first aromas of Chinese food hit him. His stomach grumbled, sparking a smile. Knowing he had a double portion of all his favorites in his hand may have been shallow, but it was the start to a good end of a potentially rotten day.

Yet, as they pulled into the driveway and hurried to unload the car before their food got cold, he realized the day really hadn't been that rotten. In fact, he'd actually enjoyed himself, and Tasha put up with his moodiness quite graciously.

Before they ate he gave a very heartfelt thank-you for how the day turned out, and dug into the food.

He couldn't believe how much the two of them ate.

All he could guess was that a single hot dog at lunch hadn't filled her up, either. Although he would never know where she put all the food she ate. While she wasn't pencil-thin like the models, she wasn't carrying around anything extra. She was well proportioned like a woman should be, with everything in all the right places.

During the past four weeks they'd shared a lot of meals together, and he saw what she ate. When she was hungry, Tasha wasn't shy. Heather, on the other hand, ate like a bird in front of him. When they went out, she probably had only half of what was served, which actually annoyed him after spending so much money on restaurant food. They were always upscale places, so it wasn't cheap. Tasha, on the other hand, ate everything on her plate, although she did pick the peppers off her pizza. Then she always ate half of his dessert until he started making sure whenever he ordered dessert, he got the same for her. Heather, on the other hand, never ordered dessert, then made him feel like a pig when he did.

Mentally, Jeff shook his head. It was almost the end of the day that would have been his wedding. Once today was over, he was going to close that door.

Never again was he going to compare Tasha to Heather, and he was going to stop thinking of what Heather would have done or not done.

It was over, and he had no regrets. In fact, he'd had more fun with Tasha in the past month than he'd had with Heather in the past year.

Until today, he hadn't exactly been fair to Tasha. She wasn't a shadow of her sister. In fact, she was the better of the two.

He had no idea why he hadn't seen that before.

"Jeff? Why are you looking at me like that?" Tasha raised her fingers to cover her mouth. "Do I have broccoli stuck in my teeth?"

He grinned. "No. You don't. You have lovely teeth. Nice and straight. You have a cute nose, too. And the nicest shade of brown eyes I've ever seen. And your hair is so pretty. It's fluffy and natural."

Tasha choked, coughed, then straightened in her chair. "Excuse me? Are you okay?"

"Yeah. I'm fine." In fact, he was finer than he'd

been for a long time. "Are you done? Would you like to put your feet up and watch a little television?"

She checked her wristwatch. "I was planning on wrapping the things we bought, but I suppose we could take a break. Sure."

On the way to the living room, she kept looking at him out of the corner of her eye. He knew she was checking him out, and he didn't care. His own eyes had been opened, and he was starting to like what he saw. A lot.

She parked herself on one side of the love seat, picked up the remote and aimed it at the television. Suddenly he was glad he left it there, instead of on the arm of the big, wide couch. They could sit on the love seat together.

"I think *NCIS* is on. Want to watch it?" She hit the button to select the channel before he replied.

"Sure." Tonight, he would watch anything she wanted, although she'd never picked any shows he hated. They seemed to like the same shows, and she also hated all the soapy dramas as bad as he did.

Before she moved to the couch, he sat beside her. "This is good. Let's just stay here."

"Okay…"

At first she was a little stiff, but she soon settled in to watch the show. He could tell she was tired because when *NCIS* was over, she didn't get up. Instead, it looked as if she was going to lean to the side and curl up with her head on the arm, which he thought was a great opportunity to see if she was going to be receptive to the direction of his new revelation.

"Come here," he said as he put his arm around her shoulders, and nudged her toward him. "You look tired. You can lean on me."

As her head rested on his shoulder she let out a big sigh. He couldn't see her face, but he would bet her eyes were closed.

In a matter of minutes, her breathing changed. She was sleeping.

Jeff couldn't help but close his eyes and enjoy it. He wasn't going to fall asleep, so he just sat there and let himself feel relaxed and content.

But it didn't last long. The sound of a blast from the television startled her awake. She jerked up, stiffened, then rubbed her eyes with both hands.

"I'm so sorry. I didn't realize I was so tired. I think I should go home."

He stood, then reached out one hand to help her up. Her eyebrows arched, but she accepted his offer and slipped her hand in his.

After he pulled her up he didn't let go as they walked to the door. However, he did have to let go as they slipped their jackets on. Tasha bent down to pick up her purse, which she'd left beside the mat. "I feel bad that you have to drive me home."

He smiled. "I don't mind." It was actually good because that meant he'd be with her longer. "How about if, this time, I pick you up for church in the morning? Going to your friend's small church is really different than what I'm used to, but I think the small group atmosphere is growing on me."

Her eyes widened. "I guess. I mean, yes. That would be nice."

She looked like a deer frozen in the headlights, knowing what was going to happen, but unable to move to get out of the way of contact.

But the contact he wanted wasn't to run her over. He wanted to kiss her.

Not tonight, though. On the day that was to have been his wedding to another woman, it just seemed wrong.

Tomorrow, that would change.

Chapter 7

Frantically, Natasha scrubbed her face of the remnants of yesterday's makeup that hadn't washed off in the shower.

He was early. She'd already hit the button to open the front door for him, and if the elevator wasn't busy, which it never was on Sunday morning, that meant she had two minutes, and he would be at her door. He'd been early before, but today he was really early. Usually she was prepared, but she wasn't now. She never needed her alarm on Sundays, but this morning, she should have set it. For the first time that she could remember, she'd slept in Sunday morning. She hadn't been up twenty minutes, and Jeff had buzzed from the ground level. Her hair was still wet from the shower, and she wasn't even close to being ready to go to church.

With Heather gone she should have slept great, but instead she'd tossed and turned all night.

It was Jeff's fault.

She'd expected yesterday would be a hard day for him, and she'd been right. All day long he'd waffled between being distracted and a bit sullen. But when he started playing with the kids' bricks at the mall, something changed. Not that he usually talked a lot, but he'd been pretty silent until they started eating supper.

When he told her she had nice teeth she'd felt like a horse under consideration for the glue factory. Then he'd acted so strangely for the rest of the night she wasn't sure what to say. Going home and straight to bed hadn't helped. She'd spent most of the night staring up at the ceiling, and when she did sleep, her dreams featured Jeff as the main attraction.

She'd barely unscrewed the wand off the tube for her mascara when Jeff's knock echoed at her door. She quickly made a swipe on each eye, didn't check to make sure it was even, then jogged to the door.

"Hi," she muttered as she opened the door. "You're earl…" Her voice trailed off and her chin nearly hit the ground as she stared at him. Instead of his usual jeans, he wore neat black dress pants…with a belt. And leather shoes, not his alleged "dress" sneakers. Today he didn't wear a T-shirt, but a button-down shirt, neatly pressed. His hair was perfectly gelled into place, and he wore one small diamond earring in his left ear, daring enough to look quite dashing. Yet still, there was something else different about him that she couldn't put her finger on, aside from looking as though he could have been a modern-day and very well-groomed pirate. Except he was going to church, not out to pillage and plunder.

She cleared her throat. "You look really nice." Which was the epitome of understatement.

"Thank you." He grinned, making him look even more dashing. "You look really nice yourself."

She doubted that. Her hair was still partially wet and she'd grabbed the first clothes she touched without much thought to coordination. She wasn't even sure if she had on two socks that matched, but she was too embarrassed to look down.

"Are you ready? I know I'm a bit early. If you haven't had breakfast, would you like to go grab some coffee and a muffin or something across the street?"

Natasha pressed her hand to her stomach. She wasn't sure if the flutters in her stomach were hunger, or panic, or maybe a bit of both. "I guess so," she said as she grabbed her purse and slipped her feet into her shoes, which gave her the opportunity to make sure that her socks did indeed match.

He waited beside her while she barely managed to control her shaking fingers as she locked up, then they made their way to the elevator.

"Why are you all dressed up today?"

He shrugged his shoulders. "I don't know. I just felt like it."

She waited for him to elaborate on why he felt that way, but he didn't.

"Do you have other plans?"

"No. Not really. I kinda thought we'd spend the afternoon wrapping what you bought yesterday."

She wanted to comment on him being way too overdressed to wrap gifts, but she was pretty sure she would get the same kind of noncommittal answer.

As they crossed the street she noticed other women staring, not at them as a couple, but at Jeff as an individual. She wanted to scream out for them to turn away, that he was hers, but he wasn't. He would never be. The way he felt about her, they would always be friends, and nothing more. After all, if there were more, he would have come up with a better compliment than saying she had nice teeth.

All hints of hunger deserted her when she realized what he was doing. Yesterday closed the chapter on his life with Heather. All ties were gone. All dates that would have been "theirs" were over and done. Today he was starting a new chapter, which meant opening himself to new relationships. He was dressed to attract women, and he was doing exactly that.

Newly single, he was out on the prowl. Maybe he would ask what she thought of potential date prospects. After all, that's what friends did. When that happened she needed to be honest without being judgmental. She'd have to pray really hard on that.

She didn't understand why he'd specifically requested they go to Dave and Ashley's small church instead of back to the big one where he'd been going most of his life. Unless it was indeed that reason—

he already knew everyone, and wanted to broaden his horizons.

Jeff held the door open for her as she entered the coffee shop. "Want to get a table, and I'll get our usual?"

She wasn't sure she wanted to leave him alone, even for a few minutes, but this was what friends did.

Being the one to sit first, she chose the spot against the wall, forcing Jeff to sit with his back to everyone entering when he returned with their breakfast. He wouldn't see who came in, and people who came in wouldn't see him, at least not his handsome face. Maybe that was petty, but more, she wasn't ready to let him go. For a while, she wanted—no, needed—to be friends without complications and without the ghost of her sister between them.

"Here you go. A cranberry muffin for you, blueberry for me. Double cream, no sugar in your coffee."

Her favorite muffin and coffee just the way she liked it. The morning suddenly got a little better.

Before they began to eat he said a short prayer of thanks. She liked that he would do that in a public place, even for something that was hardly a real meal, even though he'd barely said, "Amen," before taking the first sip of his coffee.

"So, Tasha, tell me more about this gift-giving party. How and when are the gifts handed out?"

She couldn't believe that's what he wanted to talk about, but it was a relief not to be asked for tips to attract other women. "It's a very informal thing. Bill, that's my boss, wants to keep it that way, so everyone comes. Instead of making it a formal banquet we do everything at the office so it's less intimidating. Gloria, his wife, hires a caterer, and they set up all the food in the lunchroom, but everyone is free to walk around the office. That way people can move around and talk, versus sitting at a table and being stuck with whoever is close to you for the whole event."

Jeff nodded. "That sounds like a great idea. More like a house party, but at work."

"Exactly." Natasha paused to pull her tablet out of her purse. "Now that I'm thinking about it, it's probably my boss's wife who does the decorating and gets the tree. I'll have to ask about that." She made a note for herself, then looked back to Jeff. "After everyone's finished eating, the gifts are given out, the kids run around and play, the teens go huddle in little circles, the adults socialize and after a while everyone goes home."

He smiled. "That's pretty succinct."

"That's the way it is. Everyone has a good time. Then Monday, back to work as usual." She snickered. "Although for a few days we always find remnants of the party in the strangest places. One year, we don't know who did it, but a couple of people gathered a bunch of the wrapping paper and wrapped Bill's desk. It was pretty funny."

"The celebration sounds like quite a worthwhile endeavor. I'm glad to help you."

While they ate she told him about Gloria's antics as she decorated the office as well as the Christmas tree every year. She couldn't help but smile. "The more I tell you, the more excited I'm getting about decorating my own tree. Sorry. I love the whole Christmas season. It's my favorite time of year."

He grinned back. "I'm finding that out, I think." He took the last sip of his coffee and checked his watch. "I think it's time to go. I'll drive."

It was a pretty obvious hint that today he wanted to take his car, which was fine with her. She needed the time to finish putting on her makeup, which she could do from the passenger's side.

With every red light they caught, she asked him not to look as she applied another touch to her makeup. Of course, he did look.

"Stop that!" she said with her mouth wide open as she applied mascara to one eye.

"But I have to. This is a fascinating procedure. I've never seen what it takes to get that final look."

"It's not a big deal." Although Natasha couldn't imagine that Heather would ever have let Jeff see her face without all her makeup, much less watch her apply it, especially since Heather never went anywhere without a full application of everything. Natasha usually only wore a bit of shadow, some liner, the mascara, and she only owned four shades of lipstick.

"Don't watch me. This is your fault that I didn't get this done at home."

"Fine. But I don't know why you do that. You look fine without it."

She didn't want to be the only female at church over the age of twelve without makeup. "You're still looking."

"I'm not." He turned his head forward, but she

caught him trying to sneak glances out of the corner of his eye every time he stopped, because every time she turned toward him, his head moved a little straighter to face forward.

She finished with one light to spare.

As they exited the car, she felt okay about her face, but not okay about Jeff being better dressed than her.

They met Ashley and Dave in the foyer, chatted for a bit, then made their way into the sanctuary.

Before the service began, Natasha looked around for single women, and didn't see many. Therefore this would probably be the last time they attended this small church, so when the service was over, she intended to make the most of it. This was only the fifth time they'd come here, but she really liked the people, and she especially liked the more familiar, informal way the pastor delivered his sermon. With a smaller group he made individual eye contact with probably every person present multiple times throughout his sermon. If a person nodded off, the pastor would indeed notice. But there was too much going on during the sermon.

First, the pastor had a riveting delivery that kept everyone fully attentive. She also noticed a few people who openly commented or asked the pastor questions in the middle of the sermon. He wasn't flummoxed or annoyed at the interruption. Instead, he seemed to welcome it.

She really would miss this place.

At the end of the service, she found excuses to stay in the sanctuary longer. Jeff didn't seem to be in any rush. Maybe he was just humoring her, but as all good things had to come to an end, they eventually joined everyone else in the foyer.

Instead of being beside her husband, Ashley stood, leaning on her cane, talking with a group of women. Likewise, Dave stood talking with a group of men.

Like a typical man, Jeff took a few steps toward the group of men, then stopped. He turned toward her, smiled, appearing to be waiting for her approval. Natasha nodded, so he continued on, and she joined her friend.

Conversation stopped.

Ashley turned to Natasha. "I haven't heard from you all week. I was going to ask what's up, but now I can see why."

All heads turned in unison toward Jeff, who was laughing at something someone had said.

Ashley nudged Natasha with her elbow. "What's up with that? Is something happening that you're not telling me?"

Something was going on, and she did want to talk to her best friend, but not in front of a bunch of near-strangers. "I guess he felt like dressing up."

Ashley giggled. "I guess you two have plans for lunch?"

She'd looked forward to going out for lunch with Jeff, and as far as she knew, that was still a possibility, even though they hadn't talked about it. "No, no plans."

As she spoke, Dave gave Jeff a manly slap on the back. Jeff turned around, and started walking toward her. At the same time the huddle of men split up as everyone went their separate ways. Those who had partners in their group approached behind Jeff.

Dave stepped beside Ashley. "Jeff says they have plans, so we've made a tentative date to get together with them for lunch next week, if that's okay."

"Of course that's okay," Ashley said as she again nudged Natasha with her elbow. "You two enjoy yourselves."

Before she could challenge his decision, Jeff led Natasha to the door.

"We don't have plans," she whispered so no one else could hear.

"Maybe you don't, but I do. We need to get going."

Natasha's heart dropped. All she could do was nod and follow him out without speaking. She hadn't seen him make plans with someone new, but obviously he had. It was over sooner than she thought it would be.

Jeff turned left out of the parking lot, discreetly checking the time. If they didn't catch too many red lights, they would be good.

"Why are we going this way? I thought you were taking me home?"

"I never said that."

"But I thought you said you had plans."

Jeff tried to think. He shouldn't have said anything, because he didn't want her to know.

Yet, already things weren't going as he envisioned. He'd dressed up because he wanted to look good for Tasha. He hadn't worn his earring for so long he'd worried the hole had grown in, but he thought Tasha would like it. Instead of commenting, she'd withdrawn. Unless something was wrong that she wasn't telling him. In that case, it bothered him even more, because he wanted her to be able to lean on him when she needed a shoulder, just as he'd been able to lean on her over the past month.

"I do have plans. That's why I have to hurry back home. She said the timing was important, and we got out of church later than I anticipated."

She pressed herself back into the seat. "I don't want to be a third wheel, Jeff."

"What are you talking about?"

"Nothing." Her voice quieted to almost a whisper. "Just go. You said you were in a rush."

He waited for her to say more, but she didn't. It nearly killed him to have the silence hover, but since he hadn't done a very good job of bringing her out of whatever funk she'd fallen into, he didn't want to start talking and say something to make it worse.

Hopefully she'd feel better when they got back to his place.

He turned on the CD player, knowing it was a band she liked and always sang along to.

But she didn't sing. She continued to just sit facing the window, looking kind of...sad.

He didn't know what to do, so he kept the music loud and continued driving. Maybe she'd tell him about it later, unless there was nothing he could do.

They pulled into his driveway with three minutes to spare. He wasted no time hustling her inside.

The second the door closed behind them, Tasha's eyes widened and she inhaled deeply. "What is that? Are you cooking something?"

So much for the surprise. He turned to her and grinned. "Yeah. I made you lunch."

Her eyes widened even more. He didn't think that was possible. "Really? You mean you've had something in the oven all morning?"

"Yeah. I emailed my mother and asked her for the recipe." He'd put everything together last night with his laptop set on the counter because he'd run out of toner and couldn't print it. "I gotta go get it out of the oven real fast. I don't want it to burn. Have a seat on the couch."

He hustled into the kitchen, slipped on the oven mitts, took the casserole out of the oven, placed it on the stovetop, then stood back to admire it.

His timing was perfect. It was a nice golden brown without being burned, just as he remembered. He gave himself a mental pat on the back, then turned to go back into the living room, and froze.

Tasha stood behind him, grinning ear to ear. "That smells so good, I couldn't stay in the living room. It looks delicious."

He checked his watch. "We can't cut it yet. It has to sit for ten minutes. I don't know why. It just does." And since this was his favorite brunch ever, he wasn't going to mess with success.

"Can I set the table?"

He waved one hand in the direction of the table. "Already done."

He bit his lower lip not to laugh when she gasped. He'd dug through the drawer to use matching cutlery, and two plates that were the same pattern. He couldn't find napkins, so he'd used extras he'd stashed from the Chinese restaurant, but he'd folded them so the logos were on the inside. He'd even run the dishwasher so he could use her favorite coffee mug. "The coffee should be ready. I had that on the timer, too."

"Why did you do this?"

So he wouldn't have to look at her, he turned to get the cream out of the fridge. "With all the shopping and talk of Christmas, I started thinking about Christmas at home, and one of the best things about Christmas morning was the brunch my mom always made. Mom put it together before bed on Christmas Eve, then first thing Christmas morning she stuck it in the oven to cook. It was always done when we were finished unwrapping the gifts."

He stood straight, closing his eyes to savor the memory. "Opening Christmas presents was always better when we could smell this cooking." Now, the more he thought about it, he saw the waiting period before they could eat to be a little too coincidental. The casserole needed to set after it came out of the oven. Strangely, that time was always the same time as it took to clear away all the wrapping paper and bows and packaging. He opened his eyes, turned and finished pouring the coffee. "Since you got me started thinking about Christmas, it made me remember what Christmas morning was like at our house. Then I thought, why wait? It would be a treat to make it now and share it with you. But part of the fun is the anticipation. No sampling until ten minutes. We've got eight minutes left."

She shuffled back and forth. "What are we going to do for eight minutes?"

"When I was a kid, we picked up all the wrapping and stuff. It almost makes sense to start some of the wrapping, but I know from experience it takes way longer to wrap than to unwrap. We wouldn't even get started before we had to stop. I think we should just sit down and enjoy the coffee." Maybe, if they sat with nothing to do, and no distractions, she would tell him what was bothering her. He wanted this to be a two-way relationship, and this was a good start. She already knew what was bothering him. Now it was time for her to confide in him a little bit.

She looked one more time to the casserole, then to the coffee mug. "Okay."

He found himself disappointed that she just picked up her mug and sat at the table without waiting for him to seat her. But come to think of it, he'd never seated her when they went out to a restaurant.

That would change.

The second he seated himself, she turned to the fridge and spoke without looking at him. "Did you make dessert?"

"I'm good, but I'm not that good. I bought dessert. It's one of those frozen cakes that they advertise that it's okay to stick your finger in the icing."

She turned to him. "That's really not okay. I wouldn't eat it if you stuck your finger in it first."

He thought of the times they shared the same dessert at restaurants. They were both too full to order a whole selection individually, but they often bought one piece of cake to share because they both wanted it. That made him think of movies where one member of a couple stuck their finger in the icing and the other one licked it off, which was meant to be sexy. He'd always wondered if one knew where the other's hands had last been, and there was nothing alluring about that. He'd always thought Tasha felt the same way. Now he knew. "I'm pretty sure they mean if you stick your finger in your own piece, not someone else's."

"Five minutes."

"I can see you're really hungry. I don't think it's going to make any difference to wait. Just do me a favor and stay seated. This was supposed to be a fun surprise. At least let me serve it." As he sliced the casserole and set it onto the plates, he mentally kicked himself. His previous thoughts were not that this was supposed to be a *fun* surprise. It was supposed to be a *romantic* surprise.

Maybe if he prayed for that, it might happen. But he wasn't going to pray for that now. His prayers before they ate were to be of thanks for the food and their time together, in whatever format.

Tonight his prayers would be different.

When she took her first bite, her eyes widened. As she chewed, she waved her fork up and down in the air, not to speak with her mouth full. "This is delicious," she said after she swallowed. "If that's how you grew up, with this every Christmas morning, I can see why you're such a fanatic over bacon."

"I'm not a fanatic," he said, but as the words came out of his mouth, he did realize that all his favorite foods contained bacon in some form.

"Yes, you are. You use bacon like women use chocolate. It's your comfort food."

"No...I..."

"Think about what you've eaten in the past month."

He did make himself bacon and eggs for breakfast on the weekends, and he always put bacon on his burgers. He'd even bought a bag of nonfake bacon bits to add to salads, because when Tasha came over for supper, most of the time she liked a salad with her meal, so he made sure he was prepared.

"Some of that is your fault for eating salads. But you are right. I have been eating more bacon lately."

"Don't get me wrong. I'm not complaining. This is fantastic. I'm thinking this might be the thing that started your love of bacon. In fact, this has a lot of bacon."

He felt his ears burn. "I might have used more than my mom said."

He didn't know how it happened, but for the rest of the meal they talked about cooking, then agreed to exchange a few recipes. Since she insisted, he acquiesced when she said she wanted to help clean up the kitchen. Fortunately, he'd done the entire cleanup from the casserole last night, so all they did was load the dishwasher and put the leftover casserole in the fridge.

While he made a new pot of coffee, Tasha disappeared into the spare bedroom where he'd piled the gifts she'd bought so far.

Together they wrapped everything, with Tasha being very careful to mark off the gifts on her tablet. Before he knew it, it was time to start cooking supper. Fortunately, she only laughed a little when she found out their supper was barbecued bacon cheeseburgers. After all, he had lots of bacon on hand.

All in all, the day had gone well, but it wasn't what he'd planned, or wanted.

What he wanted was to be able to kiss her goodnight. Except that when he drove her home, all the visitor parking spots were full. She just ran out of the car, called out that she would probably see him tomorrow and dashed inside her building while someone else held the door open.

Jeff smacked the top of the steering wheel, then put it into gear and headed for home.

Tomorrow he was going to see her again, but tomorrow would be different.

Chapter 8

Natasha felt her eyes drifting shut as she fell back onto the couch. Her eyes were closed by the time she landed.

She couldn't remember the last time she'd been so exhausted. A nasty flu bug had ravaged the store and half the staff was missing, both on the floor and in the office. Every person well enough to go to work needed to put in extra time to keep things running. She'd worked eleven-hour days for four days in a row, and it wasn't over yet. Tomorrow was Friday, the busiest day of the week. She didn't want to work a twelve-hour shift, but had a bad feeling it was going to be necessary. A few people were expecting to come back tomorrow, but they were still going to be significantly short-staffed, which didn't include clearing the backlog. As HR director, her position was in the office, behind a desk. But she'd been needed to work the floor, and the customer service counter.

Oblivion had nearly overcome her when a knock sounded on the door. "Tasha! It's me. Jeff. I'm coming in!" The doorknob rattled, followed by the creak of the door opening. "You should be more careful about locking your door. Any weirdo could just walk in, you know."

"Some weirdo just did," she moaned without opening her eyes. "You came a long way for nothing. I'm not moving."

Something crinkled. "But I brought food. No salad, though. Not a lot is still open so late. I didn't have many choices. So I brought burgers and fries. And nice, cold, refreshing drinks."

At this point she would welcome a burger and fries. If she could sit up or raise her arms. But she couldn't. Her body wouldn't let it happen. "How did you get in so late?" During the evening, residents often let people in they'd seen before, but now it was late, and there wasn't a lot of people going in and out at this hour.

"That woman on the third floor let me in. Is that all she does—sit on her balcony and watch the door?" His voice lowered. "I think she likes me."

"She doesn't even know you. Even though she's seen you hundreds of times, have you even met?"

"Uh. No. But I wave when she lets me in. Where can I put this? I think we should forget about going all the way to the kitchen and eat here."

She really hadn't been hungry, but now that she

could smell the burgers her stomach reminded her that she hadn't eaten since lunchtime. "I think I am kind of hungry. And really thirsty." Except she didn't know if she could get up.

"Then come and get it."

As she opened one eye, Jeff stood above her with one hand extended. Without words she accepted his offer of help and slipped her hand into his. He pulled her up gently, then released her to empty everything out of the bag.

Instead of grabbing for the burger, she picked up her drink and drank greedily. "I've never known that an ordinary drink could be so good," she murmured, then drank more.

Concern etched his features as he watched her drink. "Be careful. You must be really dehydrated if you're that thirsty. That's not good."

"I know. I've spent most of the days in customer service, so I've been talking almost constantly."

She could tell he was trying to bite back a grin... and failed miserably.

He lost control and broke out into a full belly laugh. "I can really see you talking for ten hours nonstop," he gasped, still laughing. "I'll bet you've never had so much fun in your life."

Instead of dignifying his comment with a reply, she bit into the burger. Even though it was just a burger, the flavors danced in a celebration in her mouth. Fast food had never tasted so good. And for some reason she couldn't explain, the best part of the burger was the bacon.

He was definitely rubbing off on her. Too much.

She didn't care that he was watching. She didn't want to talk. She suddenly felt so famished she barely paused between bites as she devoured the burger.

The burger was half-eaten before she could break the momentum enough to speak. "What are you doing here, anyway? I thought you had to get up at six. Isn't this rather late for you?"

He shrugged his shoulders. "Maybe. But when you texted me back I thought you sounded hungry."

She paused, midchew, then swallowed. "I was still at work, and all I said was that I was tired and wanted to go home. How did you get hungry out of that?"

He shrugged his shoulders again. "I don't know how. I just knew."

Of course she'd been hungry, but she didn't want to text about it because she didn't want to start with negatives. To do so would have made the night go even worse.

Natasha dabbed at her mouth with her napkin, then again sucked on the straw. It was down to ice, and none had melted yet.

"Want some of mine?" Jeff held out his drink toward her.

"Thanks, but I think I've had enough." She pushed back her hair, and tried to smile at him. It didn't feel quite as forced as the smiles she'd had to paste on her face for the past four days, but it was close. "I know I've been kind of negative, but I really appreciate this. Thank you."

He stood. "No worries. With that, I think I'm going

to go home now. You can finish my drink. I left it on the table."

"You're leaving?" He'd been there exactly long enough for her to eat, and she'd never wolfed down a meal so fast in her life. She glanced at the time, and yawned.

"Yes, and that's why. I'll probably see you tomorrow. Text me when you're leaving work and I'll think of something we can do."

She'd already been on the verge of rude, so Natasha quickly stood and walked him to the door. "Good night."

He stopped, and turned around to face her. "Yeah. Good night." Slowly, one hand rose. Almost hesitantly, he lightly brushed her cheek with his thumb.

Natasha felt her eyes go wide. If this had been a movie, it would have been the perfect time for the tall, dark, handsome hero to kiss the damsel in distress. Not that she was in distress. He'd fed her and she felt fine now, except for being so tired she didn't know how she was able to stand.

He looked down at her mouth.

As if he was thinking about kissing her.

For the past year, this was the moment she'd dreamed about—fantasized about—because she knew it would never happen.

But now it was here. Really happening. He was single, and available. With Heather gone, there could be no interruptions. No awkward moments. The timing was perfect.

Except, suddenly, the thought of him dating other women terrified her. He was starting to play the field, but she didn't want to play that game. She wanted to be the one—his one and only. The woman he would love and cherish for the rest of his life. She didn't want to play the usual dating games. They knew each other too well for that. She also knew she couldn't compete with the rest of the single women in the world. He'd made it clear that they would never be more than just friends. But…it looked as if he wanted to kiss her. And just thinking about it made her heart pound so hard she thought he could probably hear it.

"You have ketchup on your chin." He swiped it off with his thumb, stepped back, then lowered his hand and rubbed his thumb on his jeans. "Good night. Sweet dreams."

Before she could respond, he turned, walked out and closed the door behind him. "I'm going to stand here until I hear you click the lock."

She raised her hand, but let her fingers hover over the mechanism, not touching it. It was almost as if locking the door with Jeff on the other side would do or signify something, but she didn't know what.

"I don't hear the click," his voice rumbled from the other side of the door.

"Okay," she squeaked out, turned the knob, then slid the safety chain into place.

"Good. Good night." His footsteps sounded, fading in the distance, then she heard the hum of the elevator, signifying that he'd pressed the button.

She wasn't sure what happened, but she had a feeling that instead of sleeping, she would spend most of the night staring up at the ceiling.

"Good night," she whispered through the wood, and turned around.

He'd said he wanted her to text him when she got off work tomorrow. She wanted to take that as an encouraging sign. She really did. But what she wanted just wasn't meant to be. Instead, she would take what she could get. If friends was all they would ever be, then she would have to make the best of it, because it was better than nothing.

Jeff stood back and stared into the fridge as he packed up tonight's supper into a bag. Yesterday he'd gone by the seat of his pants and brought her burgers, which had been more practical than date-worthy. It got the job done of feeding her, but no more.

Just for good measure, he put his bottle of soy sauce into the bag, in case Tasha didn't have any. It didn't hurt to be well prepared. He had everything for a nice romantic supper, and not all of it takeout. She didn't like salad every day, but she did like vegetables, so he'd made a trip to the store to get some asparagus. He had no idea how to cook it, but he'd gone online and printed the instructions, cooked it just right, timing it for exactly four minutes in the microwave with just the right amount of butter and salt. All he had to do was throw it in the microwave once he got to her place to reheat it.

Today, he had a plan. She'd texted to say that she had to stay until the store closed, prepare the day's deposit and lock everything up. Since again she couldn't come to him, he was going to her.

As the last customer's car exited the lot, Jeff pulled in, and parked next to Tasha's, which was close to the employee exit. He turned the car off, then pulled out his phone to watch a movie he'd saved. Every time someone left, he glanced up, counting the employees, not sure how many were actually working that day, but knowing Tasha would be the last one out.

After a long gap, two people left together, one of them Tasha. As she locked up, he got out of the car.

"Hey, Tasha," he called out as he approached, so he wouldn't scare her in the dark. "It's me."

She stiffened, but didn't jump, so that was good. "What are you doing here?" she asked as she double-checked that the door was locked, and turned around.

"I don't like the idea of you going to the bank all alone so late, so I'm going to follow you. It's not a good idea to get out of the car alone with a bag of money like that." He knew she'd been nervous when she told him she had to drop the deposit off at the bank on her way home. Yes, she'd only texted, but he could tell.

Her eyes widened. "It's not exactly a bag of money—it's a locked security pouch. But with the right tools someone would still be able to get into it. Usually there are two people going to the bank every day, but with so many people sick, not today. The boss says if someone tries to rob the person who is doing the deposit, don't fight, just give it to them, but that doesn't have any guarantees. I'm glad you're going to be there."

Neither spoke as he walked her to her car and waited for her to get in. Once her door closed he jogged around his car and, as promised, followed her to the bank. Since there were no cars in the lot, she parked beside the building instead of in a designated parking spot. It took under a minute for her to unlock the metal drawer for money bags and toss the bag in, but if someone had been waiting for a victim, only seconds were needed.

She waved at him after she made sure the drawer closed securely, then hustled back in her car and began the drive home. Again, he followed her. After a few blocks, his phone rang. The hands-free option picked up the signal; it rang through the car's system, and the line opened. "Hi, Tasha," he said as he slowed for a red light. "See, I told you it was a good idea to have a hands-free system. Sometimes you do need to make calls from the car. Now you don't have to pull over." He'd called her once when he knew she'd been driving, and had been worried she'd been in an accident since it took her so long to answer. He couldn't believe it when she said she had to pull over to pick up the call. But at least she hadn't answered while driving. That would have been worse. He'd immediately bought her a hands-free system for her car, and got a friend to install it.

"I still think you spent too much money, but I do appreciate it. I'm calling because I notice you're still behind me. Your place is in the other direction."

"I'm not going home. I'm going to your house. I have food."

"Food?" He could almost hear her stomach grumble, and he wasn't sure it was his imagination.

"Yes. Good food. Yummy food. Stuff you like. Including vegetables. The whole shebang."

A pause hung over the line. "Dessert…?"

"I'm not telling. The only thing I'm going to say is that it's not the kind where you put your finger in the icing."

"I think you just told."

"Oops. It doesn't matter. You knew, anyway. I'm just not giving away any more details."

Another silence hung. "Why are you doing this?"

Because he wanted to change the parameters of their relationship. But he couldn't say that. They'd been friends for so long, he didn't want Tasha to re-evaluate things and find him missing the mark of what she wanted in a relationship. He wanted to raise it up to the next level. He couldn't take the chance that she wasn't interested in more, so he needed to get her piqued. A little at a time. Except he only had a week left to start raising the bar before Heather got home. All his feelings for Heather had gone dead and were buried, but he knew things would be very awkward when he came face-to-face with the two of them to-gether. "Because I knew you would work through your break and you'd be hungry. I can't have you waste away into nothing."

She actually laughed. Which was encouraging. "That's not going to happen in one day, but I appreciate it. You're right, I did work through my dinner break, and I am hungry. I'll see you back at my place."

The phone beeped as the car disconnected the call.

So far so good.

He pulled into the visitor parking, gathered the bag and made his way to the building. He didn't expect the woman on the third floor to be on her balcony so late, but sure enough, there she was. Holding the bag up with one hand, he waved with the other, and as always, she let him in. When he pressed the button for the elevator he wondered if when the elevator door opened maybe Tasha would be already inside, on her way up from the underground parking, but she wasn't.

As he stepped out of the elevator on the sixteenth floor, suddenly strange echoes from the past hammered at him. In his mind's eye, almost as if it was happening again, in front of the doorway next to Tasha's apartment, he pictured a couple embracing. As his feet skidded to a halt, his eyes lost focus. He stared into the empty hallway, picturing Heather and her married neighbor bolting apart when he spoke— their faces riddled with shock, then guilt.

He'd never felt so broadsided in his life. In those few seconds, he'd felt his life had come crashing down around him.

Behind him, the doors of the other elevator swooshed open. Tasha's voice echoed behind him. "And to think I was hurrying so I could get to my place to push the button to let you in." She hustled around him to her door, reached for the doorknob, then looked at him over her shoulder. "I guess that woman on the third floor was…" Her voice trailed off. She spun, then reached out and wrapped her fingers around his arm. "What's the matter? Are you okay?"

He blinked a few times to clear his head. Slowly, the picture of Heather, her lips swollen from another man's kisses, faded to a face so similar he had to blink again.

"Yeah. I'm fine." He shook his head to get the image out of his mind, but the pounding in his heart didn't disappear so fast. This was Tasha looking back at him. Innocent Tasha. Not scheming Heather.

"You don't look very fine."

"No. I'm fine. Really." He *was* fine, because Heather was behind him and his life was moving forward. With Tasha. He held up the bag. "I'm going to make us dinner. At least reheat it, anyway."

Her head tilted slightly as her gaze bored into his eyes. "Are you sure?"

"Yes. Now let's go in. I have food to prepare."

She held eye contact for a few more seconds, then opened her door.

Once inside, he closed the door behind him and made his way to the kitchen. "You go relax on the couch, and I'll get everything together," he said over his shoulder.

But instead of making herself comfortable, her footsteps echoed on the kitchen floor behind him.

"Tell me what's wrong. You looked like your dog died or something."

"I've never had a dog."

"No. But you have a pet so you know what I mean." Not making eye contact, she walked to the cupboard and removed a couple of plates while he looked for a couple of big spoons. "You looked stricken. Is something wrong?"

He opened his mouth, but his voice froze. In all the time since he'd caught Heather and her neighbor together, he hadn't really talked to anyone about it, except Tasha. He'd recapped the situation to a few people, but she was the only person to whom he'd told the ugly details.

Besides feeling as though he'd been pole-axed by Heather cheating, it had also devastated him that she hadn't been honest. If he was doing something wrong, or if she didn't love him anymore, that might have justified, at least in her own mind, a reason to be unfaithful. But she never told him anything or gave him any indication that she wasn't happy. If they had talked, really talked, and been honest with each other, they would have either mended what was wrong, or decided they weren't right for each other and both moved on.

Although, in the past month, he had thought about it and decided they weren't right for each other from the beginning. Still, it would have been better to have mutually agreed and walked away as friends than to end it as things had happened.

Now, if he wasn't honest with Tasha, that wouldn't be fair to either of them. If he wanted this relationship to work for the long term, he had to do it right. She'd asked him what was wrong, therefore he had to tell her.

If she couldn't handle it, then she wasn't the right person for him, either. He didn't want to think that was possible, but there was only one way to find out.

At least he didn't have to look at her as he spoke, if he kept his head lowered, as if he was continuing to look for the spoons. "When I got out of the elevator it was like a déjà vu moment. I started thinking about when I caught Heather and your neighbor together in the hall."

"Oh," was all she said. She paused for a few minutes, then reached for a couple of cups.

This was it. He'd already told her what he'd seen. Now he had to tell her how he felt.

"I don't know if I was more angry or devastated. I felt like I'd been run over by a truck, and then it backed over me just to be sure it was really over. I'd just been thinking about what being married to Heather would be like. My house becoming our house. Kids. At the moment I'd been thinking of getting a puppy. And then it all blew up in my face."

Jeff raised his head to see Tasha staring back at him. If he wasn't mistaken, she was holding her breath.

Automatically, his hand went to his shirt, where the tuxedo's breast pocket would have been, where he'd put his granny's heirloom ring when he took it back from Heather. Feeling it in his pocket all day and all evening at Luis and Crystal's wedding had been a biting reminder of the end of his relationship with Heather, and the failure of his dreams. "Being at the wedding was so hard. They were starting the beginning of the kind of relationship I wanted. The comfort of coming home to someone who wants me there. Being with someone who still loves me even when I'm not at my best. That also means spending my life with someone I'm going to want to be with even when she's not at her best. Someone to share the ups and downs of life. Kids. Pets. Rotten neighbors and backyard barbecues.

Someone to share the good times and the bad, just like the vows say. And in one second, it was ripped away."

Tasha swiped at her eyes with the back of her hand. "I don't know what to say," she whispered, then quickly stepped to him and threw her arms around him.

At first he stiffened, but then put his arms around her and held her against him. Fortunately, she didn't talk. She only pressed her forehead to his right cheek, tightened her hug and held on.

Now, with Tasha in his arms, he realized he hadn't been as over it as he'd thought. He'd been trying to prove, even just to himself, that he was strong and had moved on, but he hadn't. He'd pulled the plug, but not everything had gone down the drain. Today, it felt as if he'd not only cleared the drain, but also snaked it. He probably should have smiled to be thinking of Tasha as the auger of his soul. But she was more than that. He hadn't been able to talk to Luis as he'd been able to talk to Tasha.

Tasha was the best friend he'd ever had. Not only that, she was a beautiful and caring woman. He wanted to keep holding her, and kiss her to show how deeply she'd worked her way into his heart.

Tasha was a keeper. Even though she didn't say she wanted the same things as he did in a relationship, she didn't say she didn't. He could work with that.

He moved his head, just a little, and nuzzled her hair. Since it was late in the day he couldn't smell her shampoo, which he knew smelled like flowers, but her hair was still light and fluffy.

Softly he brushed her temple with his lips through her hair. He wanted to kiss her. But he didn't want to be too obvious about it. Instead of reaching up to move her hair with his fingers, he pushed her hair away with his nose until he felt her soft skin against his lips.

Now he would lightly brush her cheek, fluttering kisses against her skin until he could kiss her properly. He felt a bit of a smile coming. This moment was good, and it was going to get better.

A growly rumble interrupted his plans.

Her stomach.

He pressed his forehead to the top of her head. Here he'd been babbling about his troubles, then making plots and plans to kiss her, and all this time she'd been hungry.

He knew she'd skipped lunch.

He was an insensitive idiot.

Gently, he grasped her shoulders and stepped back. "I brought food, and it's time we ate it. Let me get everything onto the plates and in the microwave. You're going to be impressed." At least he hoped she was going to be impressed, because it was the best he could offer.

Chapter 9

"What is this?"

Jeff bit back a grin as Tasha stared at the plate he'd placed in front of her. "It's a bunch of your favorite things. Enjoy."

She continued to stare at the plate. It had taken a good part of the evening, but he'd been very careful to either prepare or buy what she liked best. It was said that the way to a man's heart was through his stomach, so he had to believe that in today's modern age, the reverse was also true. Therefore he'd made asparagus with melted cheese on top. He'd ordered Almond Guy Ding and ginger beef from the Chinese takeout. He'd cooked up a box of beef noodle Hamburger Helper, even though he couldn't understand how that would qualify as one of her favorite meals, but she'd once claimed it was. He'd baked yam fries in the oven so she couldn't complain that deep-frying canceled the goodness of it being a real vegetable, accompanied by her favorite chipotle dipping sauce. To the side, he'd added her favorite sushi combo, and made sure the rolls didn't touch the wasabi. He'd even brought a bottle of soy sauce in case the little packages weren't enough.

To top it all off, he'd bought a box with samplings of eight different kinds of cheesecake, which he knew was her favorite dessert. That was still in the fridge. She hadn't seen it yet, but he could hardly wait.

She looked up at him as he stood beside her, then raised one hand and touched her fingertips to her temple where he'd just brushed his lips. Her cheeks turned pink, she lowered both hands to her lap, then she turned her head down so he couldn't see her face. "I don't know what to say," she mumbled.

"You can say grace, and then we can eat."

She turned to watch him as he pulled out the other chair. When he smiled her cheeks darkened even more. After he took his place at the table and bowed his head she gave a short prayer of thanks for the food, then they began to eat.

"I won't be able to eat even half of this, you know."

"I know. I just wanted to make sure you had enough of everything. Whatever you don't eat we'll just put in the fridge for your lunch tomorrow."

"Lunch? This is enough food for a week."

To her credit, she nibbled first on the things he'd actually cooked. When she tasted the asparagus her eyes widened and she nodded at him while chewing, which told him that he'd done it right. She actually closed her eyes and sighed when eating the Hamburger Helper, something he really didn't understand. Next she went on to the yam fries, which he knew were a little soft, but after all, she'd been specific about them being cooked in the oven. Not that he owned a deep fryer or knew how to use one. Placing them on a baking sheet and putting them in the oven had been a total no-brainer.

Fact was, he hadn't done anything challenging, which somehow made it feel as if he was cheating, but she seemed to be enjoying his cooking, such as it was.

A few times, she reached up to brush her fingers over that spot on her temple that he'd ever-so-lightly kissed.

He wondered what she would do after he kissed her properly.

He pressed his lower lip between his teeth so he wouldn't get caught smiling, and pushed the ginger beef toward her.

Tasha shook her head. "Thanks, but I'm only going to eat a nibble of the Chinese food. I love having Chinese leftovers for a next-day lunch."

"Then I'm happy to oblige."

As they ate, since she'd been more than gracious listening to him pouring out his soul about Heather, he let her rant on about what had happened at work that day. She expounded, in detail, first about unreasonable customers, then she recounted the frustrations of other staff trying to do something they hadn't been trained to do. Many of her stories were funny, even though he didn't know the people. He supposed it was her perspective, which was always optimistic.

Between stories she complained that there was too much food, but that didn't stop her from taking just a little more of her favorite things, which was every-thing he'd brought.

Finally, she couldn't eat anymore.

He rubbed one hand over his stomach. "Now for dessert."

She covered her mouth with both hands, burped, then groaned. "You brought cheesecake, didn't you?"

"Yup."

"The kind with strawberry sauce on top?"

"Yup. And blueberry, and the chocolate kind, the mixed mocha kind, plus a few more. All the kinds you like."

She pressed one hand over her stomach. "I really can't eat another bite."

"Then how about if you go sit on the couch. I'll clean up, and then we can have dessert later."

"I don't know…"

He stood. "Go. I know you're tired. Relax. I'll pack up everything and get it in the fridge, and by the time I'm done you'll have room for dessert."

"Okay…"

He waited for the sound of the couch to squeak, signifying her descent into it, then made short work of cleaning up.

While he put everything into plastic containers and then into the fridge, he realized that he really had brought way too much food. He'd eaten his fill, as well, but there were enough leftovers to last her for both lunches and suppers through the weekend.

Suddenly he thought of the bad side to this. If she had so much food in the fridge she wouldn't allow him to take her to a restaurant because she wasn't going to let good food go to waste.

He should have thought of that sooner. But it was too late now.

Therefore he would make the best of it.

He slid a couple of pieces of cheesecake onto plates, grabbed a couple of forks, then went into the living room to join Tasha.

The television was on, but apparently, Tasha was off.

She was still sitting, but her head looked to be at an uncomfortable angle, her mouth was hanging open and she was starting to snore.

Now he knew what to expect once they got married. The thought should have stopped him dead in his tracks, but it didn't. Instead, it made him smile. All the things he'd said to her earlier ran through his mind. This was one of those moments, and it felt right. Realistically, they would have some bad moments, but most would be good, except when she picked the peppers off her pizza and left them in the box instead of throwing them in the garbage. But he could live with that.

So she wouldn't wake up with a kink in her neck, he put the two plates on the coffee table, then slipped one arm under her knees and the other behind her shoulders, and picked her up. Slowly and gently, he made his way to the bedroom, and gently laid her on the bed, which he noticed wasn't made. After he laid her down, he gently tugged off her shoes, then pulled the blanket up to her chin. When it touched her chin, she murmured and tugged it up, wiggled a bit, then stilled.

So much for his romantic evening.

Not wanting to waste the desserts, he put both back into the fridge, gave the counters one final swipe with the soapy cloth, then made his way to the door. But when he touched the doorknob, he froze.

He couldn't just leave, because he needed to lock the door.

If he locked the door, then if she had to go out, she couldn't lock her own door because he'd have her key.

He looked at the couch. He could probably fall asleep on the couch, but he didn't know if they were at that point in their relationship where he could spend the night at her place, despite being in separate rooms. If the living room counted as a separate room.

But then he got an idea. He located her keys, which were fortunately on the table beside the door and not in her purse, or worse, her pants pocket. He slipped her door key off the ring, went out, locked her door, then slid the key under the door. Knowing her purse was far away from Tasha in the bedroom and the tone wouldn't wake her, he texted that he'd slid the key under the door and she'd find it somewhere on the floor, and left.

Tomorrow was another day, and hopefully he could do something to raise the bar on their relationship then. It didn't matter what she wanted to do. Whatever she wanted, he would do.

He smiled the entire way home.

"I don't think you should get that one. It's the wrong color."

Natasha nibbled her lower lip. "It's for a dog." She turned toward Jeff, which was a mistake. The exasperation in his face nearly made her laugh. "I don't think the dog will care."

His eyebrows arched, and he waved one hand in the air toward the display. "The top thing on that girl's Christmas wish list is a dress for her dog. That means the dog is going to wear it year-round. These are all Christmas colors. You need to go over there, to the regular stock." He pointed down the aisle, where a full selection of dog clothing was displayed by size.

Regular stock. She couldn't believe that people spent so much money for something as ridiculous as dresses and shirts for dogs. Dogs had natural fur coats to keep them warm, and except for sweaters in very cold weather, they didn't need extra clothing. But obviously there was a big market for it, because the section for the dog clothing took up a third of the row.

She turned back to Jeff. "But this is for Christmas."

"Exactly. When is that girl going to get the dress for her dog?"

"At the Christmas party."

"That's my point. By the time she opens it, it will be almost Christmas. Don't give seasonal stuff at the end of the season. Have you ever got a Christmas shirt for Christmas? You get to wear it Christmas Day, then you have to put it in the closet for a whole year until after Thanksgiving when the season begins. That's no good."

As Jeff stood before her, stiff as a board, Natasha studied him. "The last time we were shopping you ended up playing with the toys instead of buying them. And now you're getting all strung out about the wrong color dog dress? Why is this so important to you?"

She expected him to get contrite, but instead he stiffened even more, and again raised his arm to point to the all-season selection of dog wear. "Because it's important to that little girl. If it's on her Christmas list, that means her parents aren't going to give her any dog outfits. If we can only give her one, then it needs to be the right one."

"We?" She wondered when suddenly they'd become a *we*. She so much wanted to be a *we* with Jeff, but everything they did together said they were just friends, except for that one moment of weakness when he'd been emotionally vulnerable. Even though she wanted more, she didn't want to read more into it than she should, and mostly, she couldn't allow herself to get her hopes up. "There is no 'we.' It's not *our* Christmas list. It's the company's. Why is this gift suddenly so personal?"

His mouth opened, but he didn't say anything. He rammed his hands into his pockets, and his cheeks flamed so bright the red reached to his ears. "Because I know what it's like to have a pet dressed out of season."

"The duck?"

He nodded. "The diapers were quite elaborate at times, and my mother always made sure to have a good variety. She once needed to have pictures taken of Daffodil as part of her advertising campaign. That was before the days most people could afford a really good high-resolution digital camera. We had to get Dilly to a studio, and since we had to take her in the car, she had to actually wear one of the diapers in public. Back then, it was bad enough to have a duck in diapers, but it was July, and she had to wear a Christmas elf diaper. Everyone who saw her laughed." His voice lowered and filled with regret. "Dilly was quite traumatized."

"The duck was upset?"

He sighed. "She's very sensitive."

Now more than ever, Natasha wanted to meet this duck.

Again, he pointed to the center display. "If the dog gets a dress, it needs to be appropriate for all year long."

"Okay. You go pick a dog dress. I'll go get the starter aquarium kit."

They had a few other pet-related requests, which she figured would be the easiest. They weren't. But soon enough they had all the pet gifts purchased, including a gift card for two complimentary fish.

"The next group is the primary and elementary level. I have no idea what to do for these. Most have no suggestions. I like it when the parents are specific." Even when her shopping partner disagreed.

Yet strangely, even though she had never spent time with this age level, they soon had a full cart, and everything on her list crossed off. Most from Jeff's suggestions.

"I can't believe the time. We're done for the day. Unless you want to start the preteen group."

Jeff rubbed his hands together. "That's when they're starting to get more interested in the electronic games. This group will be the most fun."

"My boss said no electronic games unless they're educational or have significant merit. No killing, no blood or dismemberment and nothing that glorifies bad driving."

"He eliminated the majority of what's available, but we still have lots of choices."

They managed to buy a few more gifts, but soon the small stores started to close. "All that's open now are the big-box stores. They're open late, so we can do more shopping after we eat. We need to get this all back to your house, and then we can go to my place for supper. I happen to have lots of leftovers."

"A deal I can't refuse."

It didn't take long for the car to be emptied, and everything neatly stacked in Jeff's spare room. Once they were back at her apartment, Natasha began unloading all the food containers from the fridge and setting them on the counter. "You're a good cook, you know. I was quite impressed."

With her head still in the fridge, Natasha heard shuffling behind her. She turned around with the two containers of the Chinese food in her hands and came face-to-face with Jeff—so close that when she straightened the containers she held, she touched his stomach.

"What are you doing?"

"You know that saying, kiss the cook?" As he spoke, he raised his hands and cupped her cheeks with his palms.

"Well…yes…but…"

"Then kiss the cook."

Before she could think of an adequate response, he brushed his lips against hers. Automatically her eyes closed. She felt her grip loosen on the containers, but before anything could drop from her hands, the warmth of his palms disappeared from her cheeks, and he stepped back.

"I'll take those," he said, putting them on the counter. "I have an idea."

"That's good." Because she had no ideas. Everything in her mind jumbled. All she could think about was how he could kiss her, then go back to normal as if nothing had happened. He'd kissed her. It wasn't exactly the kiss of a boyfriend, but it was on the mouth, so it wasn't the quick brush of a friend. Not that she'd ever kissed a friend before.

"I think we should make sure we have a small dinner, then stuff ourselves silly with dessert. Then we'll be on a sugar rush when we go shopping, and we'll get everything we have left in one night."

"That's not likely. I think you're just using that as an excuse to have a big dessert when we have so much food here."

"Maybe."

He began opening all the containers while she got two plates out of the cupboard. Neither spoke as they began to spoon what they wanted onto their own plates.

Overall, it seemed so…domestic. Almost friendly. But she'd never been kissed on the lips by a male friend before.

Fear of being kept firmly in the "friends only" category was the only thing preventing her from asking why he kissed her. She wanted to hang on to the hope that there could be more.

When both plates were full and heated, they said a short prayer of thanks for the food, then started eating.

Jeff ate a few bites, then looked up. "What are you doing next weekend for Thanksgiving? I'm flying out to my grandparents' place with my parents. After that I'll be spending the last night of the long weekend at my mom and dad's house. They say Daffodil is anxious to see me."

Natasha shook her head. "Sorry. We always have a huge family thing at my aunt Mary's. It's going to be a little strange, because, well, originally they'd expected you to be there, too, with Heather." She lowered her head. "By now you would have been married, but that didn't happen." She raised her head and looked back at him. "I'd like to invite you as my friend, but that would be more than a little awkward." She didn't know how to define their relationship, but they were…something.

"Yeah. I know. The day after I told my mom that Heather and I split up she called and asked if I'd go to my grandparents' for Thanksgiving. I was lucky—I got the last seat on my flight." He put his fork down and looked straight into her eyes. "I wish you could go with me."

Natasha would have liked that. Not just to meet his parents and his family, but to meet his duck. But it simply wasn't meant to be. "I guess that means that I'll be on my own for Black Friday shopping."

He visibly shuddered. "You don't really do that, do you? I don't think any discount, no matter how big, is worth the battle in a mob like that."

She gave him a weak smile. "No. I've never gone shopping on Black Friday. In fact, this year my store will be open, which we haven't done in the past. Depending on how everyone recovers from the flu, I might have to work."

He poked around at the food on his plate, not looking at her as he spoke. "I was wondering if maybe next year you might want to come with me to my parents' place. Next year is their turn to do the dinner."

She bit her tongue again, stopping herself from asking the question she was too afraid to ask.

Suddenly, things had become really awkward. "That would probably be nice, but we should discuss that next year, not now." She made a point of checking her wristwatch. "I think I'm finished. We should skip dessert and run off to get more shopping done."

"Sure. Walmart, here we come."

Chapter 10

Tonight, he would be seeing her again.

He couldn't believe it had been nearly a week since he'd last been with Tasha.

The last time he'd gone on a trip and not seen Heather for a week, he'd been fine. More than fine— he'd felt relieved because he could relax. He didn't have to worry about what he said, or if he had holes in the knees of his jeans. He didn't need to shave, and no one cared that he didn't have any gel to keep his hair in place. He'd also felt a touch of relief when the battery on his phone died and he didn't have it in his pocket while it charged.

Being separated from Tasha, on the other hand, had nearly killed him. Monday and Tuesday he didn't see her because she'd had to work killer overtime. Thanks to him, she'd been all set for dinner—the Hamburger Helper leftovers. Wednesday he'd gone to his parents' for dinner, and they'd flown away in the early evening for their Thanksgiving weekend.

He'd texted Tasha multiple times from the airport, then again when he landed. Throughout Thanksgiving and Black Friday they'd had running text conversations going until his mother threatened to flush his phone down the toilet.

When he got back to the SeaTac airport on Saturday he phoned to say he'd landed okay, and had been very disappointed to get voice mail. But then she texted him back saying she couldn't talk to him because she was with Heather. He'd left her alone on Sunday morning; after all, he'd been in church with his parents. It had been fun seeing many of his old friends, all adults now, and some married. He'd barely left the building when Tasha texted him to say that Ashley and Dave had asked about him.

He liked her friends. He liked her friends' church.

He'd phoned Tasha just before he left so he could get Dilly to quack over the phone, which she did, then he began the trip home. The only reason he hadn't called Tasha from the car to say he was almost there was because his battery died.

He wished he could have gone to her apartment, but Heather was there. That would have been awkward, so he respected her wishes.

Tomorrow, he was going to buy a new charger for the car.

As he turned the corner his heart nearly stopped.

Tasha's car was parked in front of his house, and he could see the form of someone sitting on the bench on his front porch.

Instead of taking the time to go into the carport, he stopped behind her car on the street. Leaving his suitcase in the trunk, he ran from the car to the front of his house.

"Tasha! What's wrong? I'm sorry, my battery died. Did you try to call me?"

She looked up at him with sad, mournful eyes. "I had a feeling that's what happened. Heather and I had another fight. She'd already figured out that we've been spending a lot of time together, but I refused to give her any details or talk about it. We didn't talk about it today, either. Today it was about Zac, our neighbor. She'd told me she ended things with him, but I found out that wasn't true. We had...words."

His heart tightened into a painful knot. He wished he could take her away from that, but short of getting her to elope, there was nothing he could do.

She turned and faced the blank wall, not looking at him as she spoke. "I wish there was something I could do to make her stop, but everything I say she turns around, so that it's someone else's fault that she's doing this. There is nothing that could make it right to be having an affair with a married man." She turned to face him again, and even in the dark he could detect the glistening in her eyes. "I shouldn't be bothering you with this. You've already been hurt enough by my sister."

"Don't worry. I'm over it. Nothing she could say or do could hurt me anymore."

It was true. Unless what Heather did hurt Tasha. Seeing Tasha crying over her sister's words hurt him, too.

He sat beside her on the bench, wrapped his arm around her and pulled her tight against him.

Any other time, it would have been a good moment to kiss her troubles away. But with the reason being Heather, a wall had been erected between them.

"Do you have anywhere to go tonight? Do you want to stay here? I can sleep on the couch."

She shook her head. "No. That's not right. I'll go home soon. She's probably in bed, so I can make a quiet entrance. Then tomorrow it's back to work, so I'll hardly see her." She pushed herself up, and he let her go.

"What about supper tomorrow? Will you be stuck with more overtime, or will you be free to join me?"

"I'll be fine. Everyone will be back to work, so business as usual. No more need for crazy overtime and working through lunch and dinner."

Jeff stood, too. He wanted so much to kiss her, but this wasn't the right time. "Good night, then, I guess."

She started to walk away, but before her foot touched the step of his porch, she stopped, and turned around. "Thanks for sending me those pictures of Daffodil. She's pretty cute. Was that really the duck quacking over the phone, or was that you pretending to be a duck?"

"That was Daffodil. I really don't do a fake duck

quack very well. If you have a minute, I want to show you something."

"I've got time. But I know you've got to get up early tomorrow morning."

"This will only take a minute." He quickly opened the door to let her in, then ran back to the car for his suitcase. Once he had it inside he tossed it on the coffee table, unzipped it and dug to the middle, until he touched the magazine holding the photo safely inside.

"I asked my mom for a copy of an old picture of me. This is the start of my career as a plumber."

Gently, he opened the magazine. "My parents have the original in the living room, next to a picture of me in my graduation cap from college." Now that he had a copy, he was going to frame it and hang it in the spare bedroom that he'd been using as a den, next to his diploma.

"It's me. I was in my early teens, with my first set of real tools. See behind me? That's the first waterway I built for Daffodil, and that's Dilly in front of my feet, when she was a duckling. She's still yellow in this picture. She's light brown now. She's kind of fading as she's getting older. She's a mallard, so she'll probably live up to twenty years in captivity. I don't know if old ducks go gray."

"The duck is cute, but you were cute, too."

Jeff felt himself blushing. He didn't comment.

"This is really a good photo. It's a copy, right?"

"Yes. Taken with real film. This is from the days before everyone had a digital camera."

"Can I take it to work and scan it and print a copy for myself? I promise to take good care of it."

"You want an old photo of me? Why?"

He could see her cheeks turning pink now. It was adorable. "Because it's a cute picture, and it says a lot about the man you've become."

He didn't comment on what most of the world would think of a plumber with a pet duck.

"Okay. I guess." He tucked the photo back into the magazine and handed it to her.

"Thanks," she said as she accepted it. "Now I better run home. You've got to get up earlier than I do."

"Sure." He turned so he could see her to the door when he felt the soft brush of her lips against his cheek.

Then she did exactly what she said she was going to do. She ran to the door and was outside as he stood there, frozen.

As the engine of her car started, Jeff jogged to the window and watched as she drove away, unable to wipe the smile off his face.

There was hope.

It was hopeless.

Natasha stood at the machine, waiting for it to print the picture she'd just scanned.

Even looking at a photo of him as a boy brought back visions of what she'd done last night, like repeating loops on YouTube, and now she regretted her impulsive decision. All she'd wanted to do was give him a hint of how she felt about him, so, at the time, she thought the best way to do that was to do the same thing he'd done to her—a little surprise peck on the cheek. Except, as her lips touched his skin, she felt him go stiff as a board. Instead of returning her affection, he'd frozen on the spot. He hadn't tried to kiss her back. He'd just stood there, not moving. At that moment she realized all her hopes were just delusions.

Like a coward she'd run outside before he could analyze his shock.

Apparently they would never be any more than just friends.

It was better than nothing, but not much.

From her pocket, her cell phone beeped.

She squeezed her eyes shut as she reached for it. She'd become so desperate for any contact from him, she'd started carrying her phone in her pocket instead of keeping it in her purse, in case she walked away from her desk and missed the tone that indicated a text.

She was hopeless.

She checked her phone, anyway.

I'm picking u up from work. Do not go home.

She put the picture down and texted back.

I'm not dressed up, just jeans.

The reply came back in seconds.

Me 2.

Her finger hovered over the keypad. She had no idea what he had in mind, but they were obviously not going anywhere fancy. For all she knew, they were going to the McDonald's at Walmart, because she had to do more shopping tonight.

Again, she told herself it was better than nothing, and typed her response.

K.

After a minute there was no reply, so she slipped her phone back into her pocket. She'd been holding her breath waiting for more. How pathetic.

The day went quickly because she was still playing catch-up from when so many people were off sick. Fortunately, she was able to leave on time. She headed toward the employee exit door, and sure enough, the first thing she saw after stepping out into the waning November daylight was Jeff's car.

"I still have lots of shopping to do," she said as she slipped in and fastened her seat belt.

"I understand. I thought it would save time for the two of us to go straight to the mall. If we grab a fast bite in the food court we can get more shopping done."

Natasha didn't know if she should have been encouraged that he was suddenly so enthusiastic to help her shop, or completely decimated that shopping was all he had in mind.

But for now, the shopping was important. An entire week of shopping time had been lost due to working overtime, and now she had to make up for it. The

Christmas party was in two weeks. Not only did she have to still buy half the gifts on her list, she had to wrap everything, too.

"Yes, that would work. I guess you're planning to come back so I can get my car when we're done."

"Something like that."

It was time to tackle the next age group, which was the largest, and would take more than one round of shopping.

She pulled her tablet out of her purse. "This bunch is going to be hard. Only a few parents gave suggestions. This is a group that is starting to get too old for toys, but still likes to play."

"The boys will be big into electronic games."

"The girls will be big into accessories. And games."

They looked at each other. "This should be easy," they said in unison, then smiled at each other. "Jinx!" they also said in unison.

Natasha didn't know if that was funny, or should have been scary. "You know it's not going to be easy. We can't buy the same thing for any two of them, and any games have to be nonviolent and nondestructive."

"We'll just have to take our chances." Jeff drove into the parking lot and managed to find a spot close to the mall entrance.

As he'd suggested, they went straight to the food court, picked something from the place with the shortest line and ventured into the shopping arena. By the time the store announced it would be closing they'd made some progress, but still had lots to buy.

Natasha couldn't help but notice that as they loaded

their purchases into Jeff's car, with every group of gifts, the older the children were, the more expensive the gifts, and the less room they took. The smallest gift they'd bought was a gift card for a book that would be redeemed online, for the student to read on her e-reader.

Once they were seated in the car, before he started the engine, Jeff turned to her. "Did you want to go out for coffee or anything?"

She shook her head. "No. I think we should both go home. You have to get up early, and you still have to unload the car by yourself."

"No big deal."

The whole way back to her car, Jeff complained about the shopping experience and some of the dumb things he'd seen people do, then in the next breath said that he would be happy to help her shop the next day. Because she appreciated his help, now that he was actually *being* some help, she smiled and said nothing.

When they arrived at the store where she worked, he pulled up alongside her car. Instead of simply waiting for her to get out, he turned the car off and ran out and around the car. She got out, and he stood behind her as she closed the door.

Natasha spun around. "What are you doing? You don't need to escort me. My car is right here. We're the only ones in the lot." To prove her point, she extended one arm to encompass the utter desertion.

"I know. That's *my* point." He stepped closer until they stood toe to toe, and rested his hands on the sides of her waist. "There's no one here to watch, and no one here that I don't want to see us. Just you and me."

"But—"

Before she could protest that he wasn't making sense, he cupped her cheeks and brushed a kiss to her lips. But he didn't back up. Instead, he stayed so close that she felt his smile, rather than saw it. Then he kissed her again, except this time his arms slid lower down her back and he embraced her fully as his mouth covered hers.

She melted against him, drinking in his kiss with all her heart.

It was better than she'd dreamed it would be, and she'd been dreaming a long time. He was firm, but gentle, and she'd never felt more secure than in his arms.

In the distance a siren sounded, reminding her where they were. He broke the kiss, but didn't release her. Instead, he cupped the back of her head with one palm and held her tight against him. "I've been wanting to do that for a long time," he murmured into her ear.

"Me, too," she said softly, only she wasn't going to tell him how long.

Slowly, he released her. "I'm going to follow you back to your building, and don't try to protest."

She knew better. Besides, she liked the idea of him following. "Okay. Same time tomorrow?"

She held her breath, hoping this would not be a one-time aberration.

He smiled back. "You bet."

Chapter 11

Before she arrived, Jeff needed to wipe the smile off his face.

The shopping was done. It hadn't been that bad, and the past two weeks since Tasha had got back to her normal schedule had even been the quickest two weeks of his life.

Yesterday Tasha had contacted the caterer for the Christmas party and confirmed everything. Today she'd decorated the office with some help from her workmates. Their tree was up, and they were ready for the party tomorrow.

The only thing she had to do was tell her boss that everything was complete. She'd been really excited about how well it all fit together, although she knew her boss was going to be sad about him and his wife missing the party.

And now, Tasha was going to be even happier because he had a little surprise for her, too. Actually, a big surprise. A six-foot surprise, and it wasn't him.

He almost started to pace the floor when he finally heard her car pull into his driveway.

Unable to contain himself, he ran to the door and opened it just as she stood there with her fist in the air, ready to knock.

"Hi," he said as he took her hand, led her inside and pulled her into an embrace. He planted a fast kiss on her luscious lips, then rested his hands on her shoulders. Smiling, he extended his arms, keeping his hands on her shoulders to put some space between them.

She smiled. "Hi, yourself. What was that...?" Her voice trailed off, and she sniffed. "What is that smell?" Her eyes lit up and her smile got even bigger. "I doubt you bought Christmas air freshener, so that's got to be—" She broke from his grasp and ran into the living room.

He waited for it.

"A Christmas tree!" she called out. "You bought a great big Christmas tree!"

She ran back to him, grabbed one hand and squeezed it, her feet moving almost as if she was jogging on the spot. "You bought a Christmas tree!" Then she ran back into the living room.

"I bought decorations, too!" he called out to the empty hallway as he walked into the living room.

"You told me you never put up a tree."

"I don't. I always go to my parents' place for Christmas. They have a huge tree, so I don't need one. I have a little one, about a foot tall, that I sometimes put on the coffee table, and that's all I've ever needed because there's never anything under it. But this year, I don't know why, I just felt like it." Although he suspected the reason he felt like putting up a tree this year was not just because he'd done so much Christmas shopping with Tasha. He'd never been a big fan of Christmas, but apparently Tasha's enthusiasm was rubbing off on him. "I figure we can start decorating it after we finish wrapping the gifts."

"Does this mean you really feel Christmassy this year?"

"Yeah. I do." He almost started to expound on that, but something about her expression halted his words. "Why do you ask?"

"No reason. We'd better get started wrapping the gifts. We've got a lot to do. I have a bad feeling we're going to be still wrapping in the middle of the night."

He tipped his head and studied her face. There was something he wasn't getting. He didn't know if he should ask if something was wrong. "I made us shepherd's pie for supper."

"Really? Wow, you are spoiling me. I don't know how I'm going to make all this up to you."

He wiggled his eyebrows. "I'll think of something. Let's eat."

After they started eating he got the same feeling—that there was something she wasn't telling him. It bothered him. It was almost as if he started getting flashbacks, times when he got the same kind of feeling with Heather, that there was something she was hiding from him. Whenever that had happened, he'd shaken it off, telling himself he was imagining things. As it turned out, it had been something, and it had been a big something. A something that ended their relationship and darkened his trust of future relationships.

The two sisters were as different as night and day in so many ways, but it was scary that in some ways they were quite alike. After all, they not only grew up together, they still lived together.

"So you're really feeling Christmassy, huh?" Tasha said, not looking at him.

He didn't think that was a good sign. A cold chill scurried up his spine.

"I think you already asked me that."

"Oh. Yes. I did. Well, there's nothing that makes Christmastime special like the joy of little children, is there?"

"Probably not."

She pushed her plate away, then looked up at him. "I have to tell you something."

Suddenly the delicious supper he'd made, one of his favorites, turned into a lump in his stomach. Part of him wanted to know, part of him wanted to scream and cover his ears. "What?" he asked, trying to keep his voice even.

"When I phoned my boss today and told him everything was ready for the party, he made me realize that I'd overlooked something very important."

The feeling of dread that this was going to be something personal lifted, but he still had a sick feeling that whatever she was going to say was really bad. "I can't see that anything's been forgotten. This won't really affect the party, will it?"

She nodded. "My boss always dresses up as Santa. With all the details I had to take care of, I didn't realize that I was supposed to find someone to be Santa."

"How hard is that going to be?"

"I can't ask anyone who has any children going. They would notice their father was missing. Besides, all the men want to watch their children have some time with Santa."

"Certainly you know someone."

She cleared her throat. "I know you."

It was as if his heart stopped beating. "Me?"

"There's a suit and everything. It will probably fit. You'll just have to pad it a little more than my boss. Do you have black boots?"

He gulped. "Uh…"

"If you feel strange about the beard, I'm sure there's a way to wash it."

He raised one finger in the air. "I'm not—"

"And the belt will be okay, because it's made for the costume. You don't have to worry about your own."

"—really sure—"

"Everyone in the office is really excited about Santa. It seems everyone except me was thinking about who it was going to be this year."

"—if I can—"

"There's even a photographer coming to take pictures of the kids with Santa. When the parents buy them, which most do for the grandparents and keepsakes, all the money goes to a great charity. My boss gives it to the local children's hospital foundation."

"—do that." He shook his head, doubtful she'd heard a single word he'd said. "What do you mean, take pictures? People can go to the mall for pictures with Santa."

She raised one finger in the air and shook it. "The lines are so long for those, and they're not always good. For our party, the kids are receiving gifts, and they're not in a crowded noisy mall, being hustled in and out for profit. Here, they're with friends, and everyone takes their time. I've never seen a bad picture and this is my fourth year working there." Then she did what he had a feeling she knew would get him. She gave him that puppy-dog look that made him putty in her hands, as if he wasn't already. "Everybody wins, and it's fun."

Fun for everyone except Santa, he'd bet.

"I know what you're thinking. My boss loves doing this. He has fun being Santa, and he's really sad that he's going to miss it this year. On the bright side, his mother seems to be doing much better. But since it's so close to Christmas, they're going to stay and come back on the first flight they can get after New Year's."

"That's nice," he said, for lack of anything better.

"So you'll do it?"

He sighed. "Tomorrow, right? And you absolutely can't get anyone else?"

"Sorry."

He had to appreciate that she had asked him fairly—there were no tears or scenes or begging.

"I've never done anything like this in my life." He

waited for her to say that due to his inexperience she would at least try to find someone else, but she didn't. She just looked up at him, her eyes wide in expectation.

Jeff sighed. "Okay. I'll do it. I guess in the meantime, we have a lot of presents to wrap."

He wasn't a good wrapper. Usually he paid people who set up tables in the middle of the mall to wrap his gifts. However, he had a feeling he would need the distraction.

"I don't think I've ever seen a Santa with a diamond earring before."

"Too bad. The earring stays. It's better for the kids to see the earring than the hole."

Natasha almost suggested that maybe one of her reindeer earrings would have been a better choice, but she didn't want to push her luck. She was already pushing it that he was doing this at all. Besides, once he put on the hat, which included some fake hair sewn around the brim, probably no one would see his ears.

"What did you think of the dinner?"

He grinned. "Fantastic decorating. Nice touch, with the big nativity scene in front of Santa's chair. The food was great, but kind of strange in this setting. It was restaurant-quality food, but it felt wrong eating off paper plates, sitting at someone's desk. I know you said you'd cleared the office to do this instead of renting a hall. It just didn't sink in that everyone's desks and all the computers would all still be here. This puts a whole new level to casual."

"Not everyone ate at the desks. I had both the conference room and the lunchroom open for those who wanted to use a real table."

As he stood there still grinning, Natasha thought she'd never seen him look so good. He had already changed into the Santa suit, complete with his steel-toed work boots that he'd spray-painted black. With the suit hanging loose without the stuffing in it, and holding the beard and hat in his hand, he should have looked ridiculous. Instead, she thought he was the most handsome man she'd ever seen. Earring and all. He was everything she could have wanted in the man who would be her Mr. Right.

Except, right now, he was a little wrong. "Come on. Let's get you stuffed. You're almost on."

"You make a nice elf, by the way."

"I feel ridiculous in this costume."

At that, he outright laughed. "You're kidding. Look at me, an unstuffed Santa. *I'm* ridiculous."

"You're going to get better, very soon." She spread her arms to emphasize her costume. "This is never going to change. It's done. I'm not going to look any better."

After Jeff had been so conciliatory to wear the Santa outfit, she'd felt obligated to be his helper elf, which meant she had to wear Gloria's elf costume. Except there was no helping this costume. Gloria was four inches shorter than she was, and probably twenty pounds heavier. If Natasha had to find a bright side, it was probably better that the costume be too big than too small.

She gave the tie-belt another tug. At least the pointy-toed elf slippers fit.

She reached for the beard. "Let's get this on you, get you stuffed, and you're on.

After one last check to make sure all six sacks of gifts were in order, Natasha gave her elf hat one final tug, and walked into the middle of the main office. Just as she'd instructed, everyone had gathered. It was time.

"Everyone! Listen!" she called out, loud enough for the children to hear. "What is that?"

On cue, Jeff started ringing the jingle bells from the hallway.

"Ho, ho, ho," he called out, then shook the bells a little harder.

"Who is that?" Natasha called out to the younger children, who were starting to squirm.

Jeff continued, "On Dasher, on Dancer, on Prancer, on Vixen! On Comet, on Cupid, on Donner and Blitzen!"

Natasha stopped, her mouth hanging open. This wasn't what they'd rehearsed. "Who is that? Do you think—"

"No, Rudolph!" Santa's voice boomed. "Down, boy!" A small crash echoed.

Many of the children gasped, then the room went completely silent.

That really wasn't what they'd practiced.

The jingle bells started again, the door swung open and in walked Santa, holding a big red bag over his shoulder, and the jingle bells in his other hand, ringing them over his head as he walked.

"Ho, ho, ho! Those reindeer wanted to go outside

to play, but here I am! Merry Christmas, everyone!" Jeff called out in a voice a few tones deeper than his natural baritone.

All the children let out a cheer so loud she was sure the windows rattled.

Jeff made his way to the Santa chair in the middle of the room. "What does everyone say?"

"Merry Christmas!" everyone called out, including many of the adults.

"Let's see what I've got in my bag here."

He reached in and brought out a present. "Julia Kearson! Where are you, Julia?"

A little girl in a purple dress ran to Jeff almost faster than the speed of light.

He lifted little Julia onto one knee, had a small chat with her, gave her the gift and both smiled for the camera. After Julia politely thanked him, Natasha helped her down, then waited for the next child.

Jeff was very gracious with all the children who wanted to sit on his lap, and for the older ones who didn't, he stood and put his arm around their shoulders for the photographer. Natasha ended up doing very little, not much more than running to get the next full bag when he was down to the last gift in the current Santa sack.

For the babies too small to accept their gifts, he made sure to get his photo taken with the mothers holding the babies. This worked, because he said he didn't want to pick up any children under a year old. After all the expected photos were done, Santa insisted on having a few poses taken with his helper elf. Then he posed with the photographer while some of the employees took photos of them with their own point-and-shoots.

When the photographer finally started packing up his camera, a number of the men in the group made their way to talk to Jeff, slapping him on the back or shaking his hand to thank him for a job well done.

Finally, Jeff stood. "It's time for Santa to go deliver more gifts to more children. Those reindeer should all be back now. Merry Christmas, everyone! And to all a good night!" He waved to the crowd, then left through the same door he'd come from.

The door closed, and everyone could hear him having a conversation with the reindeer. The jingle bells sounded briefly, and then everything was silent.

Knowing Santa was gone, the smaller children continued to play with their new toys, and the teens formed little groups to talk about theirs. Within a few minutes Jeff appeared at her side.

"You were great," she told him. "You really made the party a hit."

"I hate to admit it, but it was kinda fun. Just don't get any ideas. Next year your boss is more than welcome to take the job back."

For the rest of the evening they made the rounds talking to everyone. Even though she was officially off duty, she wasn't really. As the HR director it was her job to make sure everyone had a good time, and all the kids were happy.

When the party was over, people began to leave until Jeff and Natasha were the only ones left in the building. Natasha finally was able to change back into her own clothes. Then she did a perimeter check, making sure the alarm on the store was still active and had not been disturbed. When all was secure, they exited and she locked the building.

"You made a great Santa. Thank you."

He grinned. "You made a great elf. Wanna go out for coffee and doughnuts somewhere?"

Natasha yawned as she shook her head. "I can't. I didn't get much sleep last night, and today was a really busy day. I think I'm going to just go home and fall asleep."

Jeff yawned, as well. "I'm tired, too." He looked at her car, parked not far from his. They'd made three trips with both cars to get all the gifts from his house to the office, so now they only had to go their own ways home.

Before she had a chance to get in her car, Jeff stepped in front of her and wrapped his hands around her waist. "See you in the morning for church, then?"

She nodded, but before she could speak her agreement, he drew her into an embrace and his lips covered hers. She kissed him back until a horn sounded in the distance.

They both stepped back and looked from the parking lot to the street, at the taillights of the car that had honked at them.

Natasha sighed. "We've got to stop meeting like this."

Jeff shook his head. "No. We don't. But we do have to get up in the morning for church. See you tomorrow."

Chapter 12

Jeff added a bow to his mother's gift, then stood back to admire his work.

Not only could he now wrap a gift to perfection, he could also do it using a minimum amount of tape.

Tasha had helped him select the gift while they were shopping, but she refused to help him wrap it. Still, he believed he'd done a very good job by himself.

While they were shopping they'd both bought most of their personal gifts in addition to the company gifts, but he didn't have a gift for Tasha yet. Even though he'd spent more time at various malls and stores in the past month than he had in his entire life so far, he couldn't take the time to select something for her when she was with him. Or rather, when he was with her.

Sometime in the next few days he would be shopping again. Since he got off earlier, he could buy a gift for her and be home before she got off work, if he didn't dawdle. She would never know that, once again, he'd braved the mayhem at another mall.

He didn't have a lot of gifts under his tree, but he did have to admit, the decorated tree and the fresh pine scent did give the house a different feel for the Christmas season.

He liked it. She was changing him, and he liked that, too.

While he was thinking of Tasha, he walked to the window, just to watch for her when she arrived. As usual, it was raining, and the forecast was for three more days of constant drizzle, typical for a Seattle winter. Usually he didn't mind the rain too much, but as Christmas approached, he did hope for a bit of snow. Just not in rush hour.

Thinking of the white stuff, he reached to the table beside the window and picked up the snow globe that he'd bought last week while they were shopping. He usually didn't buy such things, but at the time Tasha had been bemoaning the never-ending rain, so he'd picked it up because it was related to snow. Inside was a decorated Christmas tree with gifts beneath it. Since the scene was allegedly outdoors, there was a little bunny rabbit with a Santa hat on beside the tree.

He didn't know why he'd bought such a cutesy thing. Or maybe he did. It kind of reminded him of Tasha. He'd never known anyone who reveled in the joy of the season as she did. Sometimes her expression in the mall had been just like the little bunny, looking up in awe at the star on the tree.

There had been another one exactly the same, only with a reindeer in it. He'd bought that one for Tasha. She said she put it on her desk at work, and everyone in the office picked it up and shook it when they walked by. As a plumber, he obviously didn't have a desk. He moved from job site to job site with his crew. Besides, if the guys he worked with found out, they'd laugh, and rightfully so. So instead of having his snow globe at work, he put it on the table next to the living room window.

To make his snow, he shook it, then put it back down, and watched the sparkles mixed with white snowy stuff drift down.

The sparkles hadn't all settled to the bottom when his phone sounded, alerting him to a text message.

It was from Tasha.

I will be late. Overtime. C U in an hour.

He smiled. He didn't like that he would have less time to see her that evening, but that meant he now had an hour to do a little shopping. It wouldn't even take him an hour, because he knew exactly what he was going to buy.

He put a frozen lasagna in the oven without waiting for it to preheat, and left. He made it to the mall in record time, and then saved himself more time with his plan. He had a specific destination—the jewelry store. He'd seen the perfect gift in the window, but couldn't go in to ask about it when she'd been with him. But he knew he would buy it, regardless of the price.

The line was a bit longer than he thought it would be, but he still made his purchase and returned home before Tasha arrived. Not daring to push his luck, instead of wrapping it he hid it in a dresser drawer, then hurried to the kitchen. He slipped on the oven mitts and popped open the oven to lift the aluminum foil that had covered the lasagna and made sure it wasn't scorched. It looked fine, so he removed the foil, put the lasagna back in the oven to brown, then started working on a salad to go with it.

She arrived just as the coffee was finished brewing.

"Wow. What are you cooking? It smells wonderful."

"I'm not really cooking It's a frozen lasagna. When I knew I had an hour, I put it in the oven."

"That's awesome. I'm famished."

He gave a short prayer of thanks, and soon they were eating.

"How was your day?" she asked as she spooned more salad onto her plate.

"I had a repair job on a clogged pipe that I'm not going to talk about while we're eating."

She grimaced, but didn't speak.

"But I can tell you about the razzing I got about my boots."

"I think it was a great idea to paint your boots black for the Santa gig. Did the paint start to come off already?"

"No. But that was the point. Work boots are usually

brown leather, not glossy black, so they really stood out. Someone actually called them Santa boots, so I told him that's exactly what they were. They teased me about being the old jolly guy, but it was fun. It made the day go faster."

"I wish something would have made my day go faster." She sighed, and it sounded sad.

"It doesn't matter. You're here now, eating my good cooking."

"You didn't cook this. You reheated it." She grinned. "But it's still good."

When they were done he put all the dishes into the dishwasher while she scooped the leftover lasagna into a container and put it in the fridge.

"You look tired." He bent and brushed a lock of hair off her face.

"I am. We were barely caught up from everyone being sick when we got really busy for Christmas. I think that's kind of strange. The store sells stationery and office goods—our busiest time is usually back-to-school. It's good to be busy as the economy picks up, so I can't complain. I'm just so tired."

Now that she mentioned it, he looked closely at her eyes and she did have dark circles. Thinking back, he had noticed it yesterday at church. She hadn't been her usual perky self, but he'd been a little tired, as well. He figured they were both crashing after all the work they'd done on the party.

He pulled her into a hug. "My poor little snow bunny," he murmured in her ear.

Suddenly, she froze, then began to squirm.

He released her. "Tasha?" Her face had gone pale.

"I need to leave," she said, her voice kind of croaky, and she wouldn't look at him.

"What's the matter? Do you not feel good?"

"You used to call Heather your little sweetie bunny. You just called me the same thing. Well, almost."

His mind raced, trying to think of what he'd said. "No, I didn't."

She backed up a few steps. "You did. Heather was always some kind of bunny to you. Is that what I am? Is that what I've been all along? A substitution for Heather, your little sweetie bunny?"

"No…I…" Jeff ran his fingers through his hair. "It's not like that."

She backed up again, putting even more distance between them. "I need to go."

He wanted to grab her and hold her and tell her that it was all in her imagination, but he wasn't going to make her stay against her will. That would be wrong. Helplessly, he watched as she grabbed her purse and jacket, and ran out the door without putting it on.

It didn't matter that he used to call Heather cute little bunny names.

Did it?

"What are you doing home so soon?" Heather's voice, laced with bitterness, echoed from the kitchen. "I thought you were going to Jeff's place for the evening."

Natasha walked into the kitchen. "I didn't expect to see you home yet, either." As she spoke, she tried to keep accusation and malice out of her voice. "I thought you were next door with Zac." After all, his wife and their daughter had gone to her parents' place for a few days.

While she waited for Heather to reply—not that she really expected an answer—it saddened her to think of what her relationship with her sister had become.

Over the years Heather had always been considered the smartest, the prettiest, the most likely to succeed, and Natasha had always felt second best, never able to equal her sister's achievements. As a child she'd gone through stages of resenting her sister, but as time went on she'd become as enamored with her as everyone else. When they were children, everyone—their relatives, even their parents—had excused Heather when she failed or made wrong choices. Even Natasha had overlooked Heather's mistakes. But not anymore. Heather having an affair with a married man, especially while engaged, was too big for Natasha to ignore.

"You told me you were going to stop seeing Zac. You lied to me. Again."

Heather spun around, staring at her with red eyes and rubbing her blotchy cheeks. "For your information, I did tell him that. But he told me it was over with his wife, that he was going to file for divorce. All they had to do was work out custody arrangements. He begged me not to end it, so I didn't. We kept seeing each other. Then today he told me that the paperwork has been filed. I thought that was great—we wouldn't have to sneak around anymore. But do you know what else he says now?"

A pause hung in the air, making Natasha unsure if she was supposed to respond. She wasn't even sure she wanted to hear this.

"I'll tell you what he said. He said that he's been thinking about our relationship, and since I'd been sneaking around to see him behind my fiancé's back, he doesn't trust that I wouldn't do the same to him when we're married. He said he couldn't trust me. Can you believe that?" Heather waved one hand in the air and glared at Natasha. "He was cheating on his wife, and now *he* says he can't trust *me*?"

Natasha stiffened, looked her sister straight in the eyes and gulped. "I'm not sure I could trust you, either. Face it, you were cheating, and from what I saw, you didn't seem to have any remorse about it. You weren't sorry you were doing it. You were only sorry when you got caught."

"How dare you!" Heather screeched, then ran out of the room, pushing Natasha out of the way.

Heather's bedroom door slammed.

Natasha sighed and sank down into one of the kitchen chairs. She hadn't thought her relationship with her sister could have got any worse, but apparently she'd been wrong. She'd also thought she had a great relationship with Jeff. She was definitely wrong about that, too.

She let her forehead drop to the tabletop, then covered the back of her head with her hands. Her fears about Jeff had been right all along. All her life she'd lived in the shadow of her sister—always second best, and second choice. Now she was second choice with him, as well. She'd thought things were going so well. She'd even thought he might be falling just a little bit in love with her, but obviously she'd been wrong. He'd only wanted her as a shadow of her sister.

If he could see her sister now, he sure would be in for another eye-opener.

Yet, she hoped Heather would eventually come to deal with Zac's rejection and realize the error of her ways. Personally, though, she meant what she said. She felt the same as Zac about Heather not being trustworthy. Pointing out to Heather that since Zac was cheating on his wife, he wouldn't make the best marriage partner, either, wouldn't help. But at the same time, Heather's anger over it showed Natasha that Heather wasn't going to change, or to try to make the situation better. At least, not right away.

In the silence of the room, the sound of the Muppets ringtone echoed from her purse.

Knowing it was Jeff, she couldn't answer it.

She wouldn't be a substitute for her sister any longer. It was over.

At the thought, she stood, retrieved her purse, went into her bedroom and closed the door. As she put her purse down, she pulled out the bag containing Jeff's Christmas gift. Because they'd always been together on all their shopping trips she'd been unable to buy his gift, but she'd seen the perfect thing. Since he got off so much earlier, and since she saw him every evening, she knew she wouldn't be able to go to the mall in the evenings. She'd run out on her lunch break, hoping for less of a crowd at the mall. It was still bad, but good enough that she'd made her purchase, returned to work and only been a few minutes late.

Now she was never going to give it to him.

But with less than two weeks to go before Christmas, she wasn't going to brave the crowds again to return it because all her shopping was done.

For today, the only thing she was capable of doing was to wrap the gifts she'd bought, and leave them under the tree.

Every gift except one.

Chapter 13

Jeff poked at his supper, then pushed the plate to the center of the table.

He simply wasn't hungry. He hadn't been hungry for a week and a half.

Not since Tasha had dumped him.

Numbly, he stood and walked to the living room window, not to look for her car, which he knew wasn't coming. He picked up the snow globe with the little rabbit in it, shook it, then watched as the sparkles and snow settled around the rabbit's feet.

Tomorrow was Christmas Eve, and he could envision what Christmas Day was going to be like. He'd planned on taking Tasha to his parents' home, introducing her as his girlfriend, or maybe more. He'd thought it was going to be the best Christmas of his life.

Instead, it was probably going to be the worst.

He'd left her a few messages on her voice mail, as well as dozens of text messages, but she hadn't replied to a single one.

Strange, when he split up with Heather, even though he'd felt stomped on and betrayed, he hadn't felt like this. He'd obsessed more on what he'd done wrong than the loss of not being with Heather as a person and life partner. It hadn't even taken a week, and he had moved on. After he thought about it more, he'd been relieved he'd seen the light before the wedding, not after. It had been easy to move on.

This was different. He wasn't relieved, and he wasn't ready to move on. He would never be ready.

Since Tasha stormed out he'd thought about their last conversation countless times. Now, in hindsight, he could see why she said what she did. It wasn't true. He wasn't substituting Tasha for his broken relationship with Heather. What he'd had with Heather was over, and it would never be resuscitated.

Soon after the breakup with Heather, Tasha had made him promise to not go back to the apartment she and Heather shared. He'd thought that was because it would be too awkward for Tasha to deal with the three of them in the same room, and he'd wanted to respect that.

The more he thought about it, he realized Tasha hadn't been protecting herself. She'd meant to protect him. She probably thought it would be too difficult for him to face Heather when it was clear he was involved with Tasha.

He didn't want her to protect him. He wanted Tasha to know how he felt about her. Granted, it probably would be awkward around Heather for a while, and probably even for a long time, but he didn't care.

He was going to do whatever it took to get Tasha back.

And that was going to start with a face-to-face conversation with Tasha. In front of Heather.

He slipped on his coat, locked up and left.

When he arrived at her building, all the visitor parking spots were filled up, leaving him no choice but to park across the street and half a block away. Braving the cold winter rain, he pulled up his collar and ran down the street until he arrived at her building.

Of course, today was the day the woman on the third floor wasn't sitting on her balcony watching to let him in.

He pressed the buzzer for Tasha and Heather's apartment.

Heather's voice came over the speaker. "Who's there?"

Just what he didn't want, but he would deal with it. "Is Tasha home?"

Heather's voice lowered to barely above a whisper. "Jeff? Is that you?"

"Yes. I need to talk to Tasha. Can you let me in?"

"Uh. Sure."

He waited for the telltale buzz, but there was nothing. He pulled the door handle, but it didn't open.

Again, he pressed the button. The light went on, but it didn't beep.

He couldn't help but look up, but the woman on the third floor still wasn't there.

He pressed the button another time.

Nothing.

But through the glass door, he saw the elevator open, and Heather running toward him.

She opened the door, but before he figured out what she was doing, she grabbed his sleeve and tugged him to the side. He tugged back, but she tightened her grip.

Rather than cause a scene, he allowed her to lead him away. It just wouldn't be for very long.

"I'm so glad you're here. I've wanted to talk to you for so long, but I was afraid. Words can't say how sorry I am, but I'm asking you to forgive me, anyway."

"I've forgiven you." Trust, however, was completely gone. "But that doesn't mean I want to resume our relationship. It's over. Sorry, Heather."

Her eyes welled up and tears started pouring out.

Jeff froze. He didn't know how to deal with this, nor did he want to deal with it. "Let me take you back up to your apartment."

"No," she said with a big sniffle, and her grip on his sleeve tightened even more. "I can't let anyone see me like this." She sniffled again.

Everything in him wanted to pull away from this scene, but he couldn't leave a crying woman alone in the lobby—especially a woman with whom he'd once had a close relationship, even though there was nothing she could say or do that would change his mind.

"I still love you, Jeff. I always have. I've made such a big mistake. Everyone makes mistakes."

"Sorry, but I don't love you. I love—" His voice caught in his throat.

He was in love with her sister—the right sister—the one he'd felt closest to all along, in all the ways that counted. But he hadn't really known what love was. With Heather he'd experienced the dazzle and the excitement. No matter where they went, everyone looked, and he'd felt buzzed to have Heather hanging on to his arm.

That wasn't love. That was infatuation, and he'd been very infatuated. But not in love. She'd had him wrapped around her little finger, and he'd simply been a sucker, giving her everything her heart desired, and she desired a lot. He'd spent the majority of their relationship waiting for her words of praise telling him how great he was, and how lucky she was to have him.

Jeff blinked, and stared at Heather's tears. He should have realized this before. Heather knew all the right moves to keep his attention, and he'd been suckered into every one of them.

But when it was time to talk about what really mattered, Heather was never interested. The one he'd had all those heart-to-heart talks with was Tasha, while Heather was getting ready. Tasha was the one he felt comfortable with. They shared all the typical common interests that held a couple together. He could talk to her about anything, anytime. Likewise when something bothered her, he listened, and he could usually relate, and sometimes even give her suggestions to help.

The friendship he'd had with Tasha all along was

the base on which a solid relationship, and a solid marriage, was made.

Tasha was pretty hot, too. He'd always thought she wasn't as gorgeous as Heather, but then he'd never seen Heather without all the prep work. Now that he thought about it, Tasha was hotter than Heather because she didn't need all the accessories and the hours it took to apply them.

Yet, he hadn't seen it.

He was an idiot.

He took the wrist of Heather's hand that held his sleeve in a death grip.

"Please let go. I need to go talk to Tasha. That's who I came to see."

Heather shook her head. "Natasha's not home." She sniffled again. "Please, give me another chance. I broke up with Zac. When we met he gave me such a sad story, I just wanted to help him. I don't know when it turned into more. But I saw through it all. Just a little too late. I love you, and I'll always love you." She gulped. "I promise I'll be faithful forever. I've learned my lesson. You don't have to settle for Natasha. I love you and I still want to marry you."

At her words, Jeff froze. He didn't know how he could be any more specific.

"I—" Before he could get another word out, Heather launched at him. She threw her arms around him and pressed herself to him from head to toe.

"Oh, Jeff, I love you, too!"

"But—" His words were cut off when at the same time Heather released him, then at light speed pressed her palms to his cheeks and covered his mouth with hers.

He struggled to reach between them to grab her shoulders. Just as he touched them, another voice sounded from behind him.

"What's going on here? Heather? Jeff?"

Jeff pushed Heather off, and turned to look over his shoulder.

"Tasha!"

Jeff worked his jaw, clamping his mouth shut. He wanted to shout out that nothing was happening, but even though nothing had happened, at least nothing mutual, speaking too soon could be worse than taking too long.

He'd already learned the hard way to first think of what it was Tasha had actually seen and heard.

Trouble was, he didn't know how long she'd been there.

Despite his words or protests, perception was the key.

He'd already made a mistake on that, and it had cost him dearly. He wasn't going to make the same mistake twice.

Worst-case scenario, she'd only walked in on the kiss that Heather planted on him. He had to start with that presumption, but couldn't be guaranteed.

He cleared his throat. "It's not what you think."

The second the words came out of his mouth, he knew he'd said the wrong thing. When he caught Heather and her neighbor in the hall, locked together in a lovers' kiss, the first words out of Heather's mouth had been exactly what he'd just said—that it wasn't what he thought.

Actually, what was happening had ended up being worse than what he'd thought at the time.

All he could do was look at Tasha, and pray she would believe him.

Natasha stared at the scene before her. She couldn't believe what her sister had just done.

She *had* been home and she'd seen Heather pick up the phone to answer someone buzzing at the main door. Normally she didn't pay attention, but Heather's sudden drop in voice raised her suspicions that something was very wrong. Not only did Heather hang up quickly, she left the phone slightly off the hook so it wouldn't ring again, then disappeared.

Maybe she'd just followed her instincts, but for some reason Natasha had looked out the window and seen Jeff's car parked down the street. It didn't take a rocket scientist to figure out that the visitor was Jeff, and that Heather didn't want her to know.

The question was to find out who wanted the secret meeting, Jeff or Heather.

Either way, if they decided to go back up to the apartment for privacy, Natasha had no intention of being there.

Normally she would have gone to the underground parking, but something in her made her want to torture herself and press the button for the lobby. She had to know the truth, to see it for herself, so she could tear her heart from his once and for all.

When the elevator door opened she'd seen them standing in the corner, away from the flow of people coming in or out. They appeared to be just talking, but Heather had a hold on Jeff's jacket cuff. Then the second Heather saw her coming out of the elevator, she launched herself at Jeff.

Jeff hadn't put up a fight, but he hadn't acquiesced, either. It looked as if he'd been in shock, as if he hadn't seen it coming. They'd broken apart before he really had the opportunity to kiss Heather back.

But it wouldn't be unlike Heather to launch herself at Jeff because Heather had seen her coming.

She studied her sister, who looked to be gloating beneath her tears, then Jeff, who looked as if he'd just been run over by a truck.

Natasha glared into his eyes. "Tell me, what exactly do I think?"

"Uh…I don't know. But I know what it probably looks like."

She raised one palm to silence him. "Before you speak, I'm going to tell you what I know." She turned and glared at her sister, the person she should have been the closest to in the world. "Heather, I don't know who you are lying to, but I think most of all you are lying to yourself. I don't know which story is true— the one you told me where Zac split up with you, or the one you just told Jeff where you split up with Zac."

Heather turned to Jeff, ignoring Natasha completely. "I know I hurt you. The truth is that I split up with Zac. I know I've done wrong, and I promise to be faithful from now on. I want to mend things between us. Maybe after a while, we can decide everything is better and make new plans together."

Jeff turned to her. "I'm sorry. I just can't."

At his words, Heather's eyes welled up, and the tears flowed freely down her cheeks. "I don't know why you two want to ruin my life." She sniffled. "I can't deal with this right now." Her voice changed from whining to sarcasm. "I hope you two are happy together. You losers deserve each other." She stiffened, strode to the elevator and pushed the button.

Neither of them spoke until the door opened and Heather disappeared.

Jeff turned to Natasha. "I don't know where that came from, but I really do wish her well. She's not a bad person. I just think she's made some really bad choices. Now she's got to deal with them. She's hurt a lot of people, including you."

His words stopped what she was going to say. The person Heather really had hurt the most was Jeff. She cleared her throat. "I believe she still loves you, despite what she's done. She says she's mending her ways." Although Natasha really didn't believe everything Heather had just said. In her heart she believed the version that Heather had told her earlier was the right one. Except it wasn't her place to say so to Jeff. What he chose to believe was his decision. He had been gracious and forgiving, which made her love him even more.

Except he obviously still cared a lot for Heather.

She would always live her life in the shadow of her sister. But this was one place she couldn't.

Natasha opened her purse, and reached inside. "Please don't say anything. I'd bought you something for Christmas, and even though we're not together I still want you to have it."

She didn't know why she'd wrapped it. She'd intended to take it back, but she just couldn't and had kept it in her purse. She put the small box into his hand, then started to turn away.

"Wait," he said. "Don't go. Don't you want me to open it?"

She refused to allow herself to cry. "If you want," she said, swallowing against the lump in her throat. "It might be a little girlie, so just do what you want with it."

"I need to know, what do *you* want? Is this what you want? To just go our separate ways?"

"No." She gulped. "Of course not."

He stepped closer. "Why are you leaving me, then?"

"Because I understand how you feel about Heather. I can be second choice behind her for a lot of things, but not with you."

"You're not second choice. Yes, you were second, but not in that way, only in the timing. It took spending time with you for me to realize what a big mistake I almost made. I got you a gift, too. I want you to have it, and to know the meaning behind it. If you still aren't totally sure that I can love you for who you are, not as a copy of your sister, then there's nothing I can do except try to change your mind."

Natasha gulped. "Did you say that you love me?"

He cupped her cheeks in his palms. "Yes. I did. I

bought you a gift, too. I'd like you to have it. I picked it out special for you. For us."

Her heart pounded in her chest as Jeff slipped his hand in his jacket pocket, and withdrew a small bag. He held it out to her, but when she touched it, he didn't release it. "I had plans to ask you to marry me. What I wanted was to pick out a ring, but I thought that was moving a little too fast. So don't be afraid to open it."

Her head swam with his words of love and marriage. She blinked several times to clear her eyes, and her thoughts. That was exactly what she wanted. To spend the rest of her life with Jeff. But only if his heart was really free of feelings for Heather.

She stared at the little box in her hands.

"Open it. It's okay."

She looked up at him. "Only if you open my gift at the same time."

"Okay."

Slowly, she picked off the bow, then tried to slide the ribbon away from around the box.

In front of her, Jeff sighed. "Why do women do that? Just cut the ribbon off and tear the paper. Please don't tell me you're going to save it and recycle it for next year."

Her cheeks flamed, but she laughed. "My mother sometimes does that with the large presents, never for something this small." She pulled the ribbon until it snapped, then ripped off the paper.

The box looked familiar. She didn't open the lid.

Jeff snapped the ribbon and tore the paper off the

gift she'd given him with no hesitation, then crumpled the paper and tossed it into the nearby garbage bin.

Under the paper was an exact duplicate of the box she held in her hands.

He stared at his box, then hers. "I'm not sure if I should be nervous or not," he muttered.

They opened both boxes at the same time.

In unison, they both lifted out the same thing, two halves of a golden heart, each on an individual chain.

"Wow," they said, also in unison.

"What are the chances?" she asked.

"I don't know. But I'm going to take this as a sign and ask you, anyway." He lowered his chains into the box, and covered her hands with one of his. "I love you, Natasha Brickson. With both halves of my heart. You, and only you. If you feel the same way, if you love me, if you trust me, will you marry me?"

She looked into his eyes. Big, honest eyes. She did trust him, and she did feel that all the love that shone in his beautiful blue-gray eyes was for her.

"Yes. I love you, and yes, I'll marry you."

He leaned forward and brushed a tender but short kiss to her lips, then straightened. Even though she wanted more, she didn't want to be a spectacle for the constant stream of people walking by; after all, they were in the lobby of the building where she lived. Although she suspected that wouldn't be for very long.

Before she could ask any questions, Jeff picked up one hand, then began to run his thumb up and down her ring finger.

"Originally I wanted the woman who would be my

wife to wear my granny's heirloom ring, but things have changed. Now that Heather's worn it, even though I've got it back it doesn't mean the same thing anymore. I still want you to have it, but not as an engagement ring. Wear it when you want, on a different finger, because it's still important, but in a different way now. I want to buy you a unique and special engagement ring, just for you, and I want us to pick it out together."

Her throat became tight. "I'd like that," she whispered, while she could still talk.

He enclosed her small hand in his large one. "I happen to know a great jewelry store, too. A store where I think a duplicate gift is going to get returned, in exchange for a deposit for a really nice engagement ring. What do you think of that?"

Practical. She liked that, too. All she could do was nod.

"I have another idea. I don't think we should know which set we keep, and which goes back." He released her hand and took her box, so he was now holding both, then he put his hands behind his back and mixed the boxes up. "Pick one."

She picked the one in his right hand. He tucked the other set back into the bag. "Which half do you want?" he asked as he offered her the choice.

"Are you really going to wear one of these? I know it's kind of girlie, so I was thinking you'd probably put it on your key chain or something like that."

"Gold? Banging around with my keys? No way. I'll probably get a longer and thicker chain. And I'd dare any of the guys to bug me about it. I think once they meet you, they'd stop bugging me, anyway."

This time her eyes welled up, and she couldn't stop them. "I love you so much," she choked out.

"Hold that thought. I'd like you to come home with me and spend Christmas with me and my parents. I know they're going to love you, too."

"And Daffodil?"

He smiled ear to ear. "Daffodil loves you already. You spoke to her over the phone."

"I can hardly wait."

"That's fantastic." He kissed her again. "This is going to be the best Christmas ever."

* * * * *

REQUEST YOUR FREE BOOKS!

2 FREE INSPIRATIONAL NOVELS
PLUS 2
FREE
MYSTERY GIFTS

Love Inspired®

YES! Please send me 2 FREE Love Inspired® novels and my 2 FREE mystery gifts (gifts are worth about $10). After receiving them, if I don't wish to receive any more books, I can return the shipping statement marked "cancel." If I don't cancel, I will receive 6 brand-new novels every month and be billed just $4.74 per book in the U.S. or $5.24 per book in Canada. That's a savings of at least 21% off the cover price. It's quite a bargain! Shipping and handling is just 50¢ per book in the U.S. and 75¢ per book in Canada.* I understand that accepting the 2 free books and gifts places me under no obligation to buy anything. I can always return a shipment and cancel at any time. Even if I never buy another book, the two free books and gifts are mine to keep forever.

105/305 IDN F49N

Name _____ (PLEASE PRINT) _____

Address _____ Apt. # _____

City _____ State/Prov. _____ Zip/Postal Code _____

Signature (if under 18, a parent or guardian must sign)

Mail to the Harlequin® Reader Service:
IN U.S.A.: P.O. Box 1867, Buffalo, NY 14240-1867
IN CANADA: P.O. Box 609, Fort Erie, Ontario L2A 5X3

Are you a subscriber to Love Inspired books
and want to receive the larger-print edition?
Call 1-800-873-8635 or visit www.ReaderService.com.

* Terms and prices subject to change without notice. Prices do not include applicable taxes. Sales tax applicable in N.Y. Canadian residents will be charged applicable taxes. Offer not valid in Quebec. This offer is limited to one order per household. Not valid for current subscribers to Love Inspired books. All orders subject to credit approval. Credit or debit balances in a customer's account(s) may be offset by any other outstanding balance owed by or to the customer. Please allow 4 to 6 weeks for delivery. Offer available while quantities last.

Your Privacy—The Harlequin® Reader Service is committed to protecting your privacy. Our Privacy Policy is available online at www.ReaderService.com or upon request from the Harlequin Reader Service.
We make a portion of our mailing list available to reputable third parties that offer products we believe may interest you. If you prefer that we not exchange your name with third parties, or if you wish to clarify or modify your communication preferences, please visit us at www.ReaderService.com/consumerchoice or write to us at Harlequin Reader Service Preference Service, P.O. Box 9062, Buffalo, NY 14269. Include your complete name and address.

LIDIR13R

REQUEST YOUR FREE BOOKS!
2 FREE RIVETING INSPIRATIONAL NOVELS
PLUS 2 FREE MYSTERY GIFTS

Love Inspired®
SUSPENSE

YES! Please send me 2 FREE Love Inspired® Suspense novels and my 2 FREE mystery gifts (gifts are worth about $10). After receiving them, if I don't wish to receive any more books, I can return the shipping statement marked "cancel." If I don't cancel, I will receive 4 brand-new novels every month and be billed just $4.74 per book in the U.S. or $5.24 per book in Canada. That's a savings of at least 21% off the cover price. It's quite a bargain! Shipping and handling is just 50¢ per book in the U.S. and 75¢ per book in Canada.* I understand that accepting the 2 free books and gifts places me under no obligation to buy anything. I can always return a shipment and cancel at any time. Even if I never buy another book, the two free books and gifts are mine to keep forever.

123/323 IDN F5AN

Name	(PLEASE PRINT)	
Address		Apt. #
City	State/Prov.	Zip/Postal Code

Signature (if under 18, a parent or guardian must sign)

Mail to the **Harlequin® Reader Service:**
IN U.S.A.: P.O. Box 1867, Buffalo, NY 14240-1867
IN CANADA: P.O. Box 609, Fort Erie, Ontario L2A 5X3

**Are you a current subscriber to Love Inspired Suspense books
and want to receive the larger-print edition?
Call 1-800-873-8635 or visit www.ReaderService.com.**

* Terms and prices subject to change without notice. Prices do not include applicable taxes. Sales tax applicable in N.Y. Canadian residents will be charged applicable taxes. Offer not valid in Quebec. This offer is limited to one order per household. Not valid for current subscribers to Love Inspired Suspense books. All orders subject to credit approval. Credit or debit balances in a customer's account(s) may be offset by any other outstanding balance owed by or to the customer. Please allow 4 to 6 weeks for delivery. Offer available while quantities last.

Your Privacy—The Harlequin® Reader Service is committed to protecting your privacy. Our Privacy Policy is available online at www.ReaderService.com or upon request from the Harlequin Reader Service.
We make a portion of our mailing list available to reputable third parties that offer products we believe may interest you. If you prefer that we not exchange your name with third parties, or if you wish to clarify or modify your communication preferences, please visit us at www.ReaderService.com/consumerchoice or write to us at Harlequin Reader Service Preference Service, P.O. Box 9062, Buffalo, NY 14269. Include your complete name and address.

LISDIR13R

REQUEST YOUR FREE BOOKS!

2 FREE INSPIRATIONAL NOVELS
PLUS 2
FREE
MYSTERY GIFTS

Love Inspired
HISTORICAL
INSPIRATIONAL HISTORICAL ROMANCE

YES! Please send me 2 FREE Love Inspired® Historical novels and my 2 FREE mystery gifts (gifts are worth about $10). After receiving them, if I don't wish to receive any more books, I can return the shipping statement marked "cancel." If I don't cancel, I will receive 4 brand-new novels every month and be billed just $4.74 per book in the U.S. or $5.24 per book in Canada. That's a savings of at least 21% off the cover price. It's quite a bargain! Shipping and handling is just 50¢ per book in the U.S. and 75¢ per book in Canada.* I understand that accepting the 2 free books and gifts places me under no obligation to buy anything. I can always return a shipment and cancel at any time. Even if I never buy another book, the two free books and gifts are mine to keep forever.

102/302 IDN F5CY

Name _____ (PLEASE PRINT) _____

Address _____ Apt. # _____

City _____ State/Prov. _____ Zip/Postal Code _____

Signature (if under 18, a parent or guardian must sign)

Mail to the Harlequin® Reader Service:
IN U.S.A.: P.O. Box 1867, Buffalo, NY 14240-1867
IN CANADA: P.O. Box 609, Fort Erie, Ontario L2A 5X3

Want to try two free books from another series?
Call 1-800-873-8635 or visit www.ReaderService.com.

* Terms and prices subject to change without notice. Prices do not include applicable taxes. Sales tax applicable in N.Y. Canadian residents will be charged applicable taxes. Offer not valid in Quebec. This offer is limited to one order per household. Not valid for current subscribers to Love Inspired Historical books. All orders subject to credit approval. Credit or debit balances in a customer's account(s) may be offset by any other outstanding balance owed by or to the customer. Please allow 4 to 6 weeks for delivery. Offer available while quantities last.

Your Privacy—The Harlequin® Reader Service is committed to protecting your privacy. Our Privacy Policy is available online at www.ReaderService.com or upon request from the Harlequin Reader Service.

We make a portion of our mailing list available to reputable third parties that offer products we believe may interest you. If you prefer that we not exchange your name with third parties, or if you wish to clarify or modify your communication preferences, please visit us at www.ReaderService.com/consumerschoice or write to us at Harlequin Reader Service Preference Service, P.O. Box 9062, Buffalo, NY 14269. Include your complete name and address.

LIHDIR13R

S